Sweet Haven

K.C. LYNN

Love & Peaches

K.c. Lynn
to

Published by K.C. Lynn

Sweet Haven Copyright © 2016 K.C. LYNN
Print Edition

First Edition: 2016

Editing: Wild Rose Editing
Formatting: BB eBooks
Cover Art by: Cover to Cover Designs
Cover Image by: Sara Eirew Photography
Cover Models: Tiffany Marie and Justin Edwards

Dedication

This story is dedicated to my mother-in-law, Gisele. I waited for the right book to do this. As I wrote Jase and Samantha's story, and the love they share, I often thought of you and Les. Because, if two people were ever destined for each other the way Samantha and Jase are, it's the two of you.

Thank you for always supporting me in this journey I'm on, but most of all, thank you for giving me my husband—my soul mate.

Sam and Jase are for you.

PROLOGUE

Sam

Trying to find your place in the world can be difficult.

I grew up in the best family a girl could have. My parents showered me with love and affection. My big brother protected me and showed me what it meant to be strong. And my beautiful, talented sister was my best friend.

They were my place—my home.

Then one by one they left, because their home became somewhere else. The only one I'd ever known no longer existed, and I still wasn't sure where mine was.

At one point I became lost trying to find it. It was a dark time and one I never want to live through again.

Then, one day he barged into my life—my brother's rival. With his big ego, insane good looks, and cynical attitude.

My name is Samantha Evans and this is the story of how I found my place.

My home.

My sweet haven.

CHAPTER 1

Sam

Music vibrates beneath my feet as I head up to the bar with my tray in hand. "I need three Coronas, two Jack and Cokes, and a screwdriver for table seven," I tell my friend, Zoey, who's behind the counter.

"Got it." Lining up three glasses she begins filling the order. "I can't thank you enough, Sam, for bailing me out once again. Finding reliable help nowadays seems impossible, especially on a Friday night."

I smile back at her, feeling bad about how much trouble she's had finding good servers. Zoey is one of my best friends and owns Overtime, a successful sports bar here in Silver Creek. Anytime I can help her out I do, especially since the hours don't conflict with my day job. It also keeps me busy and my mind off of things. Things I don't like to think about.

"You know I'm happy to help whenever I can. It's not like my Friday nights are ever eventful."

She chuckles, knowing it's true. "Well, thank God for that or I would have been in one hell of a bind tonight. It's going to be hard to find backup when you leave me for good," she adds, speaking of my upcoming move to Charleston. Her smile dims as she places the first two drinks on my tray. "You know I'm going to miss the hell out of you, right?"

"I'll miss you, too," I confess, my throat beginning to feel tight. "But we still have three more months together. I promise to come visit and you can come see me, too."

"I know, but it won't be the same." She pops the caps off three Coronas before putting them down in front of me and reaching for the limes nearby. "The first thing I want you to do when you get there is go to your brother's gym and find yourself a sexy fighter. If you find two then send one my way."

"Yeah right, you know how Sawyer is. The last place I'll ever find a date will be at his gym."

"Well, he's going to have to get over the whole protective big brother thing. It's time you got back on the dating train, Sam. Now that the two-timing asshole is out of the picture."

My stomach knots at the mention of Grant.

Zoey senses the reaction. "Sorry, I didn't mean to bring him up."

I shake my head. "Don't be. It's fine."

Actually, it's not fine. Nothing to do with Grant was ever fine. If I could go back and change the seven months I foolishly gave him then I would. But I can't. All I can do is move on and never let myself stoop that low again. Being with my family again will help. I've missed them so much.

Shoving my thoughts aside, I flash Zoey my perfected fake smile before turning back to the packed bar to deliver my order. It really is a great place with booths and high-top tables littering the worn hardwood floors, creating a maze of sports enthusiasts, eager to catch whatever sporting event is on for the evening. Most local sports teams come in to either celebrate their victory or drown their sorrows.

As I place each drink in front of the waiting patrons, I feel a crowd at my back as people take the table behind me. I spin around to greet them with a bright smile that dies when my gaze collides with a pair of sexy chocolate brown eyes that girls drop their panties for in a heartbeat.

Jase Crawford, my brother's sworn enemy.

His gaze blatantly sweeps down my body, making my skin tingle before slowly climbing back up to my face. I stand tall, refusing to shift under his scrutiny, knowing that's exactly what he wants. A slight smirk plays at the edge of his full lips, but there's no denying the hint of hostility in his eyes as he stares back at me.

The sexy bastard.

No, not sexy. He's just a bastard.

Well, maybe he's a little sexy…or a lot. But definitely more bastard than sexy.

Frustrated with my internal debate, I shift my gaze away from his and focus on the rest of the group. My smile returns when I see a few of the guys he's with are Jake Ryan, Cam Phillips, and Austin Hawke. They work at the fire station with him and also happen to be childhood friends of Sawyer's.

"Well, if it isn't little Evans," Cam boasts, being the first to greet me.

"Hey, guys. Good to see you."

"You, too," Austin says. "How are things?"

"Good thanks, and you?"

He shrugs. "Can't complain. How about your brother? It's been a while since we spoke."

"He's doing great. Living the dream down in Charleston with his beautiful family. He even coached my nephew's first year of hockey last season. My dad swears he's a natural and the NHL's next legend," I relay with a proud smile.

There's a grunt to my left, interrupting our conversation.

Twisting my head, I glare at those mesmerizing brown eyes. "You have something to say, Crawford?"

If he makes one rude comment about my family, I'll mess up that pretty face of his.

"Nope, I've got nothing," he answers with an infuriating smirk.

That's what I thought.

I turn to dismiss him when he speaks again. "However, I would like a drink whenever you're done bragging about your *perfect* family."

My fists clench at my sides as I get the urge to slap the smug look off his sexy face. Choosing to ignore him, I return my attention back to Austin and find his eyes lit with amusement.

"What can I get you, Austin?"

With a chuckle, he gives me his order.

I move to Cam next, then Jake, making my way around the table to everyone except Jase. Once I have their orders, it's only then that I acknowledge him.

"You?" I ask, keeping my eyes averted. If I look at him, I could end up being arrested for bodily harm...

Don't think about his body, Sam.

"Well, thanks for finally asking me, Peaches."

My teeth grind at the nickname. He started calling me that the last few times I've run into him, but I have no idea why. It drives me crazy.

"I'll take a bottle of Bud."

When I start away he gently snags my wrist, stopping me in my tracks. His touch ignites an inferno throughout my entire body that burns from my head right down to the tips of my pink painted toenails. I drop my gaze where his fingers sear my skin before meeting his eyes, getting lost in the deep dark irises.

"And while you're at it, fetch me a menu."

I snap back into myself at his condescending tone, narrowing my eyes in anger.

Oh, I'll fetch him something all right.

Yanking my hand back, I head to the bar, slamming my tray down with a resounding smack.

Zoey looks up at me from where she makes a Caesar, her brows arched. "You all right?"

"I'm fine, why?" I grind out.

"Because your cheeks are flushed and you look like you're about to rip someone's head off."

"I am."

"Who?"

I shake my head. "Don't worry about it."

Concern pinches her expression. "If someone is giving you problems, Sam, just say the word and his ass is gone."

"No, it's fine," I assure her. "It's just Jase Crawford. That man drives me crazy."

She looks over my shoulder with a smile. "Ah, the sexy fire boys are in the house." Her fingers dance in the air as she gives them all a wave before bringing her attention back to me. "What happened with Jase?"

"He pushes every single one of my buttons."

"I wish he would push mine, especially the one between my legs."

As irritated as I am, I can't help but laugh. By the smile she gives me it's clear that was her intention.

"Don't ever let him hear you say that. He doesn't need his ego fed."

"True, but you have to admit he's hot enough to be a little arrogant. They all are."

"Hey, whose side are you on here?" I ask defensively.

"Yours. Always yours, but there shouldn't be any sides with the two of you, Sam. The problem is between him and Sawyer. It always has been."

"Exactly. He hates my brother so of course that affects me, too. And let's not forget our fathers can't stand to be around each other either."

Though, I've never understood why.

"Okay. I get it. I do," she says. "I can assign Tara to their table. I'm sure she'll have no problem serving a group of sexy firefighters."

"No!" I reject her offer immediately. "I'm not going to give him the satisfaction. I can handle him."

"You sure?"

"Absolutely."

She shrugs. "Okay, let me know if you change your mind."

"I will. Thanks."

Relaying their order to her, I wait while she fills the drinks. When the sound of laughter cuts through the steady noise of the bar, I glance behind me and see it's coming from their table. Unable to stop myself, my eyes immediately lock with Jase's. He gives me a cocky wink that has my blood heating to a dangerous temperature.

Turning back around, my eyes land on the bottle of Tabasco next to Zoey. A smile dances across my lips as an idea forms. "Pass me that, will ya?"

"What?" she asks, bringing her attention up to me.

I gesture to the sauce next to her. "That."

Once she hands it to me, I unscrew the top and tap a few drops into the bottle of Budweiser before soaking the rim with it.

"What the hell are you doing?"

"Fighting fire with fire," I tell her, feeling my smile spread.

"Oh shit. I don't think that's a good idea."

"Don't worry about it. It's just a little hot sauce. No harm. No foul."

She shakes her head but a chuckle escapes her. "Fine, but you're on your own with this one."

"Don't worry. I can handle it," I promise before pointing over her shoulder. "I need a menu too, please."

After she passes me one, I slide it under my arm then lift my tray and head back over to their table. My smile is radiant as I stop beside Jase first. I place his beer down in front of him then take the thin booklet from under my arm.

"Your menu," I announce, slapping it against his chest with as much force as I can without losing my tray of drinks.

He flashes me those dimples of his that girls swoon over. "Why thanks, Peaches."

"No problem, *sugar plum*," I toss back, making him and everyone else at the table chuckle.

We'll see how funny he thinks it is a minute from now.

I keep him in sight as I deliver the rest of the drinks. When I place the last one in front of Cam I see him grab the beer and tilt the bottle to his lips.

Within seconds what fills his mouth spews right back out. "What the fuck?" he sputters, wiping his lips with the back of his hand.

"Is there a problem with your beer, Jase?" I ask, nothing but sweet innocence coating my tone.

His furious eyes snap to mine. "What the hell did you put in here?"

"Just the Tabasco you ordered. That was you, wasn't it?" I ask, tapping my bottom lip. "Or maybe it was someone else…"

Laughter erupts around the table; Cam's being the loudest of all. "This is the best fucking thing I've ever seen."

Jake gives me a nod of approval while Austin reaches over the table, giving me his fist. "There's that Evans's spirit."

Feeling proud of myself, I tap knuckles with him. Jase, however, looks less than amused. He looks downright pissed.

With more courage than I feel, I saunter over to him, placing my hands on either side of his chair. Leaning in close, I try to ignore the way his alluring masculine scent invades my senses. "I tell you what, Crawford. If your mouth is a little hot why don't you head up to the bar and *fetch* yourself some water."

Something dark flashes in his eyes before his gaze drops to my mouth. A gasp parts my lips when he hooks a hand behind my neck and pulls me in closer. So close that I can feel his warm breath whisper across my lips.

"You just waged a war, little girl. I hope you're prepared."

Swallowing past my dry throat, I try to calm my wild heartbeat, refusing to let him rattle me. "No, Jase, I just ended it." I give his freshly shaven jaw a gentle slap. "Now, let me go get you another beer…minus the hot sauce."

I grace him with the same wink he gave me earlier then move out from under his hand and walk away. My steps are slow and faked with confidence as I make my way back over to the bar. The air that's been trapped inside of my lungs finally releases once I reach the counter.

"Jesus murphy. What the hell was that?" Zoey asks, fanning herself. "I thought you were going to slip him the tongue."

"So did I," I admit on a heavy breath.

Seconds pass before we burst into a fit of laughter.

"God, Zoey." My hand moves to the back of my neck where I still burn from his touch. I swear the guy is some sort of magician to have that kind of effect on women.

"I told you he was hot."

"Yeah, he's hot. And arrogant and infuriating and—"

She raises her hand with a chuckle. "I get the point."

Shaking my head, I try to erase the last five minutes from my mind…and body. "Get me another bottle of Bud, please. I'll pay for it before I leave tonight."

She quirks a brow at me but does as I ask, popping the cap.

"Thanks." Swiping the bottle, I start back to their table. My steps falter when I see a few girls have joined them, one being Stephanie Taylor. The town bicycle and Jase's ex. She sidles up next to him, wrapping her arms around one of his biceps. He doesn't reciprocate but he doesn't push her away either.

A sick feeling forms in the pit of my stomach. A feeling that should have no bearing on me whatsoever because Jase is no one to me. I can't stand him.

So why the hell do I care?

Because I don't like Stephanie. It's her fault Sawyer and Jase hate each other. She made Sawyer think she and Jase had broken up when he slept with her. However, I must admit that Sawyer was stupid to mess with her in the first place. Everyone knows that girl is nothing but trouble.

Arriving at their table, I avoid eye contact and place the new beer down in front of Jase before picking up the old one. My plan is to keep moving—until the bitch speaks.

"When did you start working here?" she asks in a patronizing tone. "I thought you are a babysitter."

I'm a preschool teacher and she knows it, but I don't bother correcting her. Instead, I turn back around and ignore the way she clings to Jase. "My friend needs extra help tonight to make sure whores like you aren't spreading their diseases."

Muffled chuckles sound around the table.

Her eyes narrow in hatred. "Go back to the playground you're always at and leave places like this for real women."

"I'd pick those children over the likes of you any day. Their IQ is much higher and so is their class." I start away, refusing to waste any more time on her, but what she says next has me freezing in place.

"How's your family, Samantha? Oh wait, that's right, they all left because they couldn't stand you."

I fight like hell against the pain that infiltrates my chest. She's wrong. She doesn't know what she's talking about. Logically, I know this, but it doesn't stop it from hurting. She knew exactly where to hit.

"Shut the fuck up, Stephanie."

Surprisingly, the harsh words come from Jase. A few of the other guys start in on her too, but I don't stick around to hear it. I continue on, not wanting her to see how much her words hurt.

For the next hour, I avoid their table like the plague and hand it off to Tara. I can't trust myself to be near that bitch. I'm not usually a violent person but for her I'd make an exception.

Spotting a few empty tables in the back that need clearing, I grab the bottle of cleaner and my dishtowel then head that way. As I'm wiping one down I sense eyes burning into my back. Looking over my shoulder, I find Jase watching me. There's something in his gaze as he stares at me, something I've never seen from him before. I can't pinpoint what it is but it's captivating, like an invisible magnet pulling me in. I'm so caught up in it that I don't realize I'm not alone until it's too late.

"Hello, Samantha."

Every muscle in my body stiffens; dread twisting my stomach at the regal voice. Straightening, I turn to find Grant. The last person on earth I want to see. I'd even take bicycle bitch over him.

He takes me in from head to toe, his nose wrinkling in distaste. Not surprising. My long, wavy hair, jean skirt, and black tank top would never be up to his standards. Good thing I don't give a shit about his standards anymore.

Of course, he is in immaculate condition. He's dressed in his usual business attire with not one strand of his light brown hair out of place.

Obviously, another *late night* at the office.

Crossing my arms over my chest, I take a step back from him, feeling my back meet the wall, and quickly realize I'm cornered. Definitely not something I want when dealing with him.

"What are you doing here?" I ask, skipping over any pleasantries.

"I came to see you. I had no choice since you've been refusing my calls." His voice is calm but there's no denying the anger in his crystal blue eyes. An anger that used to scare the hell out of me and still does, if I'm being honest, but I'd never let him know it.

I will never give him that power over me again.

"We have nothing more to say to each other."

"Yes, we do. Now this needs to stop, Samantha. You're acting like a foolish adolescent."

My teeth grind at the way he uses my full name, scolding me like a child.

"It's time to get over your tantrum and—"

"This is not a tantrum," I snap. "We're over, Grant."

"The hell we are!" Fear grips my chest as he steps closer to me, his eyes flashing in fury.

Stay calm, Sam. He won't touch you. Not here.

Not ever again.

"Everything all right?"

My head snaps to the side, unexpected relief swamping me at the sight of Jase.

"Fine," Grant answers before I can, his tone icy. "We're having a conversation, if you don't mind."

"Actually, we're done." I seize the opportunity to slide out from the corner I'm in and move closer to Jase. "Grant was just leaving."

At the feel of his furious gaze on me, my eyes drop to the floor, silence hanging heavily in the air.

"Very well," Grant says, sounding a lot calmer than I know he is. "We'll talk about this another time, Samantha."

I shake my head but it's pointless since he's already turned his back and walked away. A shaky breath escapes me, my hand resting on my queasy stomach.

I should have known he would show up sooner or later.

I clue in to the person standing next to me, feeling his eyes boring holes into the side of my head.

"You want to tell me what that was all about?"

"It's nothing," I mumble, my throat burning with humiliation that it had to be him who showed up at the right time.

"Really? That's why you're shaking right now?"

I look down at my trembling hands, angry with myself for letting Grant rattle me so much. Gripping the washcloth tighter, I move to walk past him, but he doesn't let me.

His fingers wrap around my arm in a gentle grip. "Sam…"

"Just let it go, Jase." Pulling my arm free, I walk away and head into the back for some privacy. It takes me a few minutes before I'm able to find my composure again. When I return to finish my shift, I try not to think about Grant, but it proves impossible. So many emotions storming inside of me, especially regret.

Once the place dies down, Zoey offers for me to go home. I take it because I'm not being much use right now anyway. My head is not in it anymore and I think she senses that. It's obvious she never saw Grant come in; otherwise, she would've had a field day with his ass.

After giving her a hug, I grab my jacket and purse then pay for Jase's beer that I sabotaged. Before leaving, I glance over at their table one last time but don't see him there. My first thought is he left with Stephanie, but I spot her by the far corner near the bathroom. I give the rest of the guys a wave good-bye then head out into the dark night.

As I round the corner of the building where my car is parked, I come to a hard stop when I see Grant standing there, waiting for me.

CHAPTER 2

Jase

As soon as I walk out of the bathroom, I'm met by Stephanie. "There you are. I was wondering where you went," she purrs in what she deems a sultry voice but it only makes my teeth grind.

The bitch has been annoying the fuck out of me all night.

"What do you want?" I ask, my tone bored as I look above her head, seeking out the one girl who has invaded my every thought tonight.

Her hand moves to my chest as she presses her fake tits against my arm. "Come home with me."

I finally meet her gaze. "Been there, done that. Remember, Steph?"

She gives me a seductive smile. "I've never forgotten. We could have that again if you give us half a chance."

I don't think so. Not now, not ever.

"I'll pass… Just like the last fifty times."

Ignoring her scoff, I continue on and go search for the other girl who drives me crazy but in a completely different way. I look for wavy blonde hair and long toned legs that are meant to be wrapped around a man's waist. Not mine of course. No fucking way. No matter how much my dick wants her and her peach scent.

It will never happen.

Unable to find her anywhere, I head up to the bar where Zoey is. "Hey, where's Sam?"

She quirks a brow at me. "Why do you want to know?"

"Because I need to talk to her."

She eyes me for a solid minute, clearly not trusting my intention.

Can't say I blame her.

"I told her to go home," she finally answers. "She seemed off. You wouldn't know anything about that, would you, Jase?"

Yeah, I know something but it's not what she's thinking.

Instead of telling her that, I offer my thanks then move for the door, unable to shake this feeling in my gut. Sparkling green eyes flash in my head, eyes that were wide with terror not even an hour ago. I don't care how much she played that shit off. I know what I saw. She was fucking terrified of whoever that douche bag in the expensive suit was.

Stepping out into the warm night air, I scan the parking lot, hoping to catch her.

"Get in the car, now!"

"No. I told you we're through, Grant. Now, leave me alone."

Recognizing her shaky voice, I dart left, my strides quick but not fast enough. The moment I turn the corner, I hear the smack. It echoes through the air as her face snaps to the side, her hand resting against her delicate cheek.

What the fuck?

I'm stunned for only a second. Rage pumps ruthlessly through my veins, putting me in motion. My feet pound the cement, matching the furious rhythm of my heartbeat. Charging past Sam, I take him to the ground. My fists are hard and fast as I deliver blow after blow to his face, feeling the tiny bones shatter.

"How do you like it, asshole?" I grind out, relentless with every hit.

"Jase, stop!" Sam's voice is distant, echoing in my ears along with the rage that has consumed me. "Please. You're going to kill him!"

Her cry of fear finally penetrates the angry haze that surrounds me. Stopping my blows, I fist his dress shirt and yank his mangled face up to mine, my chest heaving with fury. "If you ever come near her again, I'll fucking kill you."

One eye glares up at me, the other one already swollen shut, but it gives me no satisfaction. He deserves so much more.

"This isn't your business," he spits out, blood sputtering from his mouth in the process.

"I've made it my business. Don't fuck with her again or next time I won't let you walk away."

Releasing his shirt, I allow Sam to pull me back. After he struggles to his feet, his attention strays to Sam. I step in front of her, blocking his view. "Get the fuck out of here before I change my mind and finish you now."

He straightens his suit as if this gives him a measure of dignity before climbing into his Lexus and driving off.

I turn back to Sam, her hand resting against her cheek once again.

"Let me see." I reach for her wrist but she backs away.

"It's okay. I'm okay," she breathes shakily, not sounding okay at all. I'm not sure if she's trying to convince herself or me.

"Are you sure?"

She nods, a little frantically, and it's not long before the first sob shatters from her chest. Covering her face with her hands, I watch her shoulders tremble, her pain gutting me from the inside out. This time when I reach for her she doesn't back away. My arms engulf her delicate body as she buries her face in my chest, soaking my shirt with her tears.

"It's all right," I lie, my hand coasting up and down her slender back. It's not all right and it isn't going to be. At least not for that piece of shit.

When minutes have passed, I take a small step back and slip a finger under her chin. "Let me see, Sam." I keep my voice calm when I feel nothing but rage.

She allows me to tilt her face up, her usual sparkling green eyes now filled with pain and something that looks a lot like shame. That alone makes me want to beat the shit out of the fucker all over again, but even worse than that is the angry red welt that marks her smooth cheek. A mark that she should never bear.

With anger thick in my veins, I keep one arm around her and use my other to dig my phone from my pocket then hit the contact I have for the police station.

"Silver Creek Police Department."

"I need to report a—"

My phone is ripped from me before I can finish the sentence. Sam takes a step back, ending the call.

"What the hell did you do that for?"

"No cops," she says quietly, her voice gruff with emotion as she hands me back my phone.

"What are you talking about? You have to report this."

She shakes her head. "It won't matter."

"How can you fucking say that?"

"Because they won't believe me," she snaps.

"Of course they will. I saw it happen. You have the mark to prove it for christ's sake."

"Will you trust me on this? I know what I'm talking about. I've been through this enough times."

The admission forces another surge of heat through my veins, fury blinding and searing me.

It's obvious she regrets letting that information slip. Shaking her head, she moves past me to her car door.

"Sam, wait. Don't go," I say, coming up behind her.

"I just want to be alone right now."

I watch as she fishes around in her purse for the keys and notice her hand shaking like a leaf as she retrieves them. So much so that they fall to the ground. "Shit!"

She's about to bend down to grab them but I'm faster and swipe them up before she can. "I'll take you home."

"No. It's okay. I'll be fine." She sniffles, reaching for the keys, but I keep them in my tight fist.

"I'm not letting you drive like this. So you either let me take you home or I'll call you a cab."

I'm hoping like hell she lets me take her because I won't sleep tonight unless I know she made it home safely.

She finally meets my gaze, that ever-present spit of fire I normally see from her now burning in her eyes. I hold her stare, refusing to back down.

She relents with a tired sigh. "Fine, whatever. I don't have the energy to argue with you right now."

Thankful for the small victory, I climb in the driver's seat of her practical, conservative car and try to ignore the peach scent that infiltrates my senses as soon as I enter.

Other than rattling off her address to me, she remains quiet. The entire drive she stares out her window, the back of her hand swiping across her cheeks to eliminate her tears. The silence is probably a good thing, because the more time that passes, the angrier I become.

Who the hell is that asshole to her? It's obvious he was once a boyfriend, but why the fuck would she shack up with a prick like him? I might not know her well but the Samantha Evans I've encountered over the years doesn't seem like the type of girl to put up with any shit. Hell, just tonight I thought she was going to rip my balls off for the way I gave her a hard time. She had no problem dishing it right back to me. So, how the hell did she end up with a guy like him? And where the hell is her family in all this?

The thought reminds me of the comment Stephanie made to her earlier tonight. She had her back to us but everyone at the table could feel the pain pouring off her. It pissed me off, not only toward Stephanie but also her whole family, and I didn't need another reason to not like them.

It shouldn't matter to me. It's not my business. *She's* not my business, but I can't seem to help it.

As we pull up to her apartment complex, she directs me to her parking stall. Climbing out, we meet in front of her car, and I hand her back the keys.

"Thanks," she says softly, her gaze fixated on the ground. "How are you going to get home?"

"I'll walk."

"You can take my car if you want, and I can pick it up tomorrow."

"It's fine, I'll walk."

She nods, her eyes remaining on the ground. "Listen, Jase. I would really appreciate it if you didn't tell anyone what you saw tonight."

I stare down at the top of her blonde head, my jaw flexing in irritation. "Really, Sam? That's all you have to say?"

She finally lifts her head, her emotional eyes narrowing in anger. "What do you expect me to say? Do you really think this is easy for me?"

"I want you to say that you're going to report him and press charges."

"I told you it won't matter! What part of that don't you understand?"

"I'm trying to but it makes no sense. I fucking saw it happen. I'll give a statement."

"Your statement doesn't matter. He's very influential, Jase."

"Oh bullshit."

"It's true."

"You're really just going to let him get away with it? What if he comes back?"

"I'm sure he won't. Not after what you did to him. His ego is too bruised."

"Do you really want to take that risk?"

She expels a frustrated breath. "Look. I really don't have much choice. Trust me, going to the police won't help. If anything, it could make it worse. Besides, I only have a few more months left here then I'm gone."

I tense at the last bit of information. "What the hell are you talking about?"

"I'm moving to Charleston this summer to be closer to my family," she whispers, my chest restricting at the information for some damn reason. "When that happens, I'll never have to see him again."

"Yeah, instead it will happen to someone else, but at least you're in the clear." It's a low blow and I know it, but I'm too pissed off to care right now.

Her teeth grind but there's no denying the dark pain that enters her eyes. "I don't expect you to understand."

"And I didn't expect you to be the type."

Shit! Why can't I shut up?

"What type is that?"

"A doormat." The words are out of my mouth before I can stop them, regret tearing through me the second they're said.

"Fuck you," she seethes, jamming her finger in my chest, but tears shine bright in her emerald eyes, striking me right down to my core.

"Sam, listen I—"

"No, *you listen*. You don't know me, or anything about me. You have no idea who I am. So you can take your judgment and shove it up your ass!" Spinning in place, she takes off inside, a sob falling from her in the process.

"Fuck!" My fist connects with a tree but the pain shooting up my arm does nothing to dull the burning sensation I have in my chest. I think about going after her but decide to cut my losses before I fuck this up even more.

I walk around the building, making sure that asshole's car is nowhere in sight, then start my long ass walk home. During the hour that passes, the fresh air does nothing to ease the fire raging inside of me, because the entire time all I can see is her sad green eyes.

A sadness I helped cause.

CHAPTER 3

Sam

The next morning I lie in bed and stare up at my ceiling, shame and humiliation burning inside of me as I think about the night before. Running into Grant was bad enough but having Jase witness what he did just added salt to the wound.

I didn't expect you to be the type.

What type is that?

A doormat.

His comment really hurt but it wasn't an unfair assessment. Once upon a time I was weak. A time where all I wanted was to belong to someone, to find my place like everyone else had in my family. It was time. Jesse and Sawyer had grown up and moved on well before my age. They didn't rely on my parents to be their home forever and it was time I had done the same.

So when the charming Grant Fleming, the most eligible bachelor in Colorado, asked me out when he could have his pick of women, I was swept away. I've always been in the background, especially in my family. Sawyer and Jesse are the stars, their charismatic personalities and talent always shining bright. It's one of the many things I love and admire about them but that's never been me.

When Grant started showering me with romantic gestures, I fell hard and fast. I thought I had finally found my place. Did I need a person to find it? No, but ever since I was a little girl all I ever wanted was to grow up, fall madly in love, and have a family. It was my destiny. I felt it all the way down to my bones, still do. I thought Grant possibly could have been that person but I learned quickly that he wasn't.

The first time he put his hands on me, I left him. I had locked myself in my room for three days straight and cried until there were no tears left. Then I gave him a second chance because I believed he was remorseful. He seemed so wrecked by it and promised it would never happen again. I didn't think I would ever be *that person* but he was very persuasive. The hits were few and far between but he was really good at causing pain in other ways. He always knew what to say that would hurt the most. Always used my love for my family against me and told me I was immature for still living at home.

It didn't help when I overheard my parents talking one night about wanting to move closer to Sawyer and Grace but they didn't want to leave me behind. It was then I knew I had to move on. I refused to burden them any longer, even if they didn't see it that way.

I really did want to go with them but I had to try it on my own first. It was hard to say good-bye. I've missed them so much but that's all about to change. Soon, I will be reunited with them. If that makes me weak then so be it. Some people can live away from their family, and that's great, but it's not me. I want them in my life. I want to see my niece and nephew on a regular basis. I want to be able to watch my parents grow old together. If only I could convince Jesse to move down there too, but I know that won't happen. She loves LA and is happy where she is but she makes a point to visit as much as possible so that helps.

Pulling myself from my thoughts, I reach for my phone off the nightstand and call my parents' house, needing to hear their voices now more than ever.

My dad answers on the second ring. "Sammy! How's my girl?"

His cheerful, husky voice brings a smile to my face but it dims at the dull pain in my cheek. A reminder of the disaster that ensued last night.

"Hey, Daddy. I'm good. Just waking up and missing you guys so thought I would check in."

"We miss you too, honey. Won't be long now until I get to see my girl's pretty face."

"I'm counting down the days," I tell him honestly.

"The kids are real damn excited, too. Hope has lots of recipes planned for you and wait until you see our boy on skates this fall. I'm tellin' ya, he's a natural. Just like your brother. The kid is going places."

Another smile graces my lips. "Like father, like son. I can't wait to see him in action and give that little princess a hug."

"And I can't wait to hug mine," he says, melting my heart. "I've missed you, Sammy."

His gruff words are both soothing and painful. "Me too, Dad. So much," I whisper, my throat thick with tears.

"You okay?"

"Yeah. Just tired is all. I helped Zoey out last night at the bar."

"Oh yeah? How did that go?"

"Good."

At least it started out that way...

"I ran into Cam, Jake, and Austin there. They asked about Sawyer."

"They've always been good boys. Are they still playing?"

"I think so. I believe they have a team with the fire department. I think Jase Crawford started it. He was also with them last night," I add, though I'm not sure why I feel compelled to mention him.

"I'll bet he did." The hostility in his words comes as no surprise.

"Dad, can I ask you something?"

"Of course."

"Why don't you get along with the Crawfords? I mean, I get why Sawyer and Jase don't get along but what happened with you and Mr. Crawford?"

"Nothing happened per se," he starts. "The guy has always just been a goddamn hothead. Thinks his shit don't stink and no one is as good as his son."

Sounds a lot like someone else I know.

It's on the tip of my tongue to say that out loud but I bite it back, knowing he would deny having anything in common with a Crawford.

I love my dad and brother more than any man on this earth but it's no secret they have egos that outweigh their good sense. However, their hearts are much bigger and that's what's most important.

"Why do you want to know?" he asks, suspicion thick in his tone. "He hasn't been giving you problems has he?"

"No, no. Nothing like that." The problems Jase gives me I can handle...most of the time. "I just wondered. Seeing him last night made me think of it."

"Well, if he ever does, you just let me know. I'll take care of it."

Little does he know, the last person I need protection from is Jase Crawford. If not for him showing up who knows how far things would have escalated with Grant.

The thought crashes back down on me, souring my mood. "I promise, Dad. It's all good. Anyway, I better get in the shower. Tell Mom I said hi and give her a kiss for me."

"Will do. I love you, Sammy. Call again soon."

"I love you, too. Bye." Hanging up, I climb out of bed and head to the bathroom, my heart heavy once again. I avoid looking in the mirror, not wanting to see the mark I know will be there.

The shame and pain that lingers is reminder enough.

CHAPTER 4

Jase

Today was supposed to be my day off. Yesterday was the end of my rotation but I traded with Declan to stay on one more day because I knew *she* would be coming here—the girl who has stolen my every thought.

Sam is bringing her preschool class in today for a field trip, and I have to see her. I haven't been able to get her grief-stricken eyes out of my head. I have to know she's okay. I hate that I care, I don't want to but it seems the organ in my chest has a mind of its own when it comes to her.

Once they arrive, Cam is the one to greet them at the door and lead them into the back room where the demonstration is set up. A pile of kids all cram their little bodies through the entryway, excited smiles on their faces. Austin and Jake stand at the front of the room while I stand off in the back corner.

Sam walks in next, her smile radiant, giving me a chance to take in my first full breath since leaving her devastated almost a week ago. However, all that air is stolen once again as I take her in from head to toe. From her peach colored shoes, to her conservative white knee-length skirt and matching peach tank top that's tucked in, showing every one of her perfect, slender curves in the classiest way possible.

Seriously, what is with this chick and fucking peaches? She smells like them, dresses in the color. Hell, even the natural tone of her perfect full lips is fucking peach. I'll bet she tastes as good as one, too...

Don't go there, Crawford. You don't need to be sporting a hard-on around a bunch of kids.

The pep talk proves pointless the moment her sparkling green eyes meet mine. The connection strikes me to my fucking core, shooting straight to my dick.

Shit.

It's short lived when her smile dims along with her gaze. Her eyes widen, surprised that I'm here. I'm not sure why she would be. She knows I work at this station. Unless, she checked to see if I was going to be here. If that's the case then I'm busted.

I hold her stare and try to ignore the way my chest tightens along with my jeans. How the hell I can have so many conflicted feelings about one chick, I have no idea, but it drives me fucking crazy. I just need closure from the other night. Once I know she's okay and that guy hasn't bothered her again, I can move the hell on.

Eventually, she dismisses me and turns her attention to the class, slapping on that perfected smile of hers. "All right, boys and girls. Pick a spot on the floor." She gestures to the space in front of her, lining up all the little rug rats so they can see over one another. One of them laughs as she tickles them, to make more space in front. "Good. Now, crisscross applesauce."

The entire place becomes silent as they all cross their legs and fold their hands on their laps.

"Wow, you guys are good listeners," Cam praises.

"I have the best students," Sam says, her genuine smile lighting up the whole damn station. It's clear to see this is her element and she enjoys her job.

"I can see that. Thanks for coming in, guys. I'm Firefighter Cam. This ugly dude to my left is Firefighter Austin."

They all giggle at his introduction.

"The other next to him is Firefighter Jake, and the one in the back is Firefighter Jase."

I give a brief wave as every single head cranes back to me.

"Today, we're going to teach you about fire safety and prevention while also showing you some cool equipment. You ready?"

They cheer enthusiastically.

Austin grabs Sam and the other lady she came in with a chair so they have somewhere to sit. As Jake and Cam begin the safety instruction, my thoughts and attention are on Sam, wondering how I'm going to get her alone for a few minutes to talk to her.

Every once in a while she glances in my direction then quickly skirts her eyes away when her gaze collides with mine. It gives me satisfaction to know she's not completely oblivious to me.

Next, Cam goes through the equipment we wear, kneeling next to the gear. "Do any of you know why we have our uniform set up like this?" he asks, pointing to the pants that are inside out with the boots in them ready to go.

All the kids shake their heads, their attention riveted on him.

"Because it's the fastest way for us to put them on when we have to leave in a hurry," he explains. "You see, when that bell rings we have to stop whatever we're doing and be super-fast. We can't waste even a second struggling with our gear and equipment. People are depending on us."

"Because dey need you to save deir life," a little girl says.

"That's right." Cam nods. "Or their house or whatever we can help with. Like I said earlier, we are first responders too, so sometimes it can be a car accident or something else we're needed for. It's not always a fire. Do you want to see how the equipment works?"

They all nod excitedly.

"Do you guys want to see Ms. Evans in it?"

"Yeah!" They cheer.

"Oh no." Sam laughs, shaking her head. "I'm good. You go ahead and put it on," she tells him.

He gives her a smirk that makes me want to punch him in the face. "Come on. Do it for the kids."

"Pleease, Ms. Evans." A bunch of them plead.

"Oh, all right." She stands from her chair and walks over to Cam, giving him a playful elbow for volunteering her.

He chuckles then directs her to step into the boots and begins suiting her up. A foreign feeling brews inside of me, hating that he gets to stand next to her and touch her…

Jesus, what the fuck is wrong with me? Since when do I get jealous of anyone?

As he suits her up he explains how the uniform is made of two-layer fabric designed to repel heat and wick away any moisture that gets inside.

"What happens if you have to pee?" one girl asks.

Cam looks down at the kid, clearly not expecting the question. "Well, we have to hold it. There are no bathroom breaks when you're fighting a fire."

"Have you ever peed your pants?" another one asks, all the kids snickering at the question.

"Yeah, have you, Firefighter Cam?" Sam asks, biting back a smile.

"Nope, but Firefighter Jase has," he lies with a smug grin.

My eyes narrow at him while all the kids burst into laughter.

Asshole.

Once everyone gets it out of their system he moves on, putting the air tank on Sam's back.

"Holy smokes this is heavy," she grunts.

All the kids snicker as she stumbles but Cam is there to catch her. It jacks up my annoyance another notch.

Feeling like I'm completely losing it, I step out of the room and head down the hall to the kitchen. I pour myself a cup of coffee and take some time to screw my head back on straight.

This is not how it's supposed to be. We thrive on pissing each other off. I like to press her buttons as much as she likes to press mine, that's how it's always been. But since the night I saw that bastard hit her, my perception of her turned into something else. Maybe because the girl I always saw as another spoiled Evans, the sister of my enemy, isn't who I thought she was. There's more to her than I realized. But no matter what, nothing will ever change that she's an Evans and always will be. I need to remember that. Just the thought of that smug brother of hers heats my fucking blood.

The sound of clicking heels down the silent hallway breaks into my thoughts. Sam enters into the kitchen with a smile on her face that fades the moment she sees me. She comes to a hard stop just inside the room.

"Sorry," she says quietly, looking around. "I thought this was where the bathroom is."

"Next door down." My chest constricts with panic as she steps out of the room to continue on. "Sam, wait."

She stops but keeps her back to me, her shoulders tense. I move to stand in front of her but she refuses to look at me.

"Please, don't do this to me, Jase," she whispers. "Not here. Not when I have my kids with me."

I blow out a breath, the pain in her voice making me feel like shit. "I don't want to fight. I just...I want to make sure you're okay."

"I'm fine. This *doormat* can take care of herself."

Guilt flares in my gut, knowing I deserve that. "I didn't mean it, Sam."

"Yes, you did, but I don't care what you think of me. I never have." The lie flows seamlessly from her lips. We both know she cares as much as I do.

She makes an effort to leave again but I grab her wrist to stop her. That same jolt of electricity I always get when our skin meets sears me from the inside out. She looks down at my hand before bringing her eyes up to mine, a million emotions reflecting back at me.

Releasing her, I take a step back. "Listen, before you go I need to tell you something and you're probably not going to like it."

"What?" she asks nervously.

"I spoke to a friend of mine at the police department."

Her eyes flash with fury. "You did what?"

I hold a hand up. "Just hear me out. He's a good guy. I trust him. I don't know what happened when you reported it before. It's not my business but—"

"Exactly, Jase. This isn't your business."

"The hell it isn't," I snap. "The past might not be but what happened the other night is, and I'm not going to let that bastard walk away like it never happened."

She looks away from me, her teeth grinding.

I collect a breath, not wanting this to end the way it did the other night. "Look. My friend paid him a visit and warned him to stay away from you. Hopefully, he listens, but if not, Sam, if you need help or even change your mind about reporting him, you can trust Denver. He's one of the good guys. He won't turn his back on you." I hold out his card to her. "Just think about it."

She takes it, her eyes finally meeting mine again. "Why are you doing this?" she asks softly. "Why do you care? It's no secret you hate me."

I step forward, backing her against the wall. My hands pin on either side of her head, the sweet scent of peaches invading my senses and wreaking havoc on my self-control.

Her eyes are wide as she stares up at me.

"We love to hate each other, Sam." Actually, I don't hate her at all but it's better for the both of us if I don't shred that façade. "Believe it or not, despite what your brother has filled your head with about me, I'm not a complete asshole."

I dip my head in closer, trailing my nose along her satin cheek. She inhales sharply as I torture us both, bringing my lips to her ear. Why do I do this? I have no idea. Maybe because I know it will be the last time I'm ever this close to her.

"I'd never hurt you," I whisper, my lips grazing her earlobe. "But if someone ever does again and I hear about it…I'll fucking kill them."

Feeling her quick breaths skim across my jaw, I push from the wall and walk away before I end up doing something stupid, like taste those tempting lips of her.

I've spoken my piece. Said what I had to say, the rest is up to her. Now I can move on and not give her a second thought.

At least I'm going to damn well try.

CHAPTER 5

Sam

A few days later, I pull up to the fire station with a plate of home-made chocolate chip cookies and a thank you card my class made for the station. My heart beats erratically in my chest, knowing whom I will encounter on this visit. I don't know if I'm excited at the prospect of seeing Jase again or terrified.

Probably both.

After a lot of thought, I decided to take a leap of faith and call Sheriff Cunningham, hoping I could trust him. Turns out I could. Not only did I file a report on Grant but I also put a restraining order on him.

Sheriff Cunningham was as nice as Jase said he would be. He never judged me and kept everything quiet like I wanted. He also said he would investigate the officer who turned me away the one time I did try reporting Grant. I had found out after he and Grant were friends.

I feel good about the decision I made. I just hope everything remains private. The last thing I want is for this to get back to my family or friends. I'd hate for them to know just how weak I once was.

Austin is in the front lobby, carrying a large box, when I walk in. "Hey, Sam," he greets me with a handsome smile.

"Hi. I hope it's okay I stopped by unannounced like this."

"Of course it is. We're always open to the public," he says, easing some of my worry.

"Good, because I wanted to bring you guys these." I hold up the plate of cookies with the piece of construction paper taped to the saran wrap. "My way of saying thank you for having us the other day. We had such a great time. My kids haven't stopped talking about it."

"Glad to hear. We enjoyed having you guys," he says. "Come on, everyone is in the back."

I follow him into the kitchen to see Cam, Jake, and a few guys I don't know. Disappointment pings in my chest when I see there's no sign of Jase, but I quickly shove it aside, refusing to acknowledge it.

"Little Evans, miss us already?" Cam belts out as he stands from the table and strides over to greet me.

"I sure did," I tell him, feeding his ego. "I also came by to bring you guys these." I hand him the plate of cookies and handmade card. "Thanks for being so amazing to my kids and me the other day."

"Hey, anytime. It was fun. Even when I was asked how I piss with my gear on," he says with a smirk.

I giggle, my cheeks turning pink at the memory. "Yeah, sorry about that. Kids have no filter at that age."

"Don't worry about it. It's nothing I can't handle." Lifting the saran wrap, he snags a cookie and pops the whole thing into his mouth. "Did you make these?"

"Of course."

"They're fucking good," he compliments with his mouth full, making me smile.

"Don't eat them all, asshole." Jake snags the plate from him and places it on the table for everyone else.

"Can I get you something to drink, Sam?" Austin asks. "A coffee or soda?"

"Coffee would be great, thanks."

As he pours me a cup, Jake introduces me to Declan and Rubin, the other two guys in the room.

"They're rookies, not as cool as us...yet," Cam teases, knocking Declan's hat off his head before getting shoved back in return.

"Well, rookies or not, it's nice to meet you both," I say with a smile while accepting the steaming cup from Austin.

"You, too," Declan greets back with a nod. "Sorry we missed you and your class the other day. We heard it was eventful, especially after you left."

His smirk has my mug pausing halfway to my lips. "Why? What happened after I left?"

"Oh nothing," Cam says, his tone amused. "Just that Crawford wanted to kick my ass for flirting with you."

Shock pulses through me, swearing I misheard him. "What? Why on earth would he do that?"

He shrugs. "You tell me. He's been acting different since that night at Overtime. He disappeared around the same time as you without so much of a word to anyone. When he found out you were coming in for a field trip he switched his shift with Declan. Then later got all growly with me for flirting with you."

Why would Jase care? He hates me.

We love to hate each other, Sam.

The memory of him crowding me against the wall with his strong body suddenly invades me. I haven't been able to stop thinking about it. My body still burns from it.

All the guys stare at me, waiting for an explanation, but I find myself speechless. I don't know what to say or think.

"Be careful, Sam," Austin warns, genuine concern thick in his tone. "If your brother hears something is happening with you and Crawford, he will bring down the goddamn world in his wrath."

"Nothing is going on between Jase and me," I tell them.

By the smirk Cam flashes me, it's clear he thinks I'm full of it.

"Good," Jake says. "If I were you, I'd keep it that way. I like Crawford, he's a good friend and so is your brother, but those two have a lot of bad blood between them and always will."

"Thanks to Stephanie," I grumble.

"Nah. That was just the final straw. Those two have never gotten along, even before her. But that bitch definitely didn't help things."

"Who knows," Cam cuts back in. "Maybe Sam will be the one to end this rivalry between them once and for all."

Yeah, right.

They don't know the real reason why Jase disappeared that night. It's not even close to what they are thinking. Instead of telling them that, I steer the conversation in another direction. "So, are you guys ready for the big fundraiser this Saturday night?" I ask, mentioning the auction they agreed to do for Zoey.

They all groan, sounding less than enthused by it.

"I still can't believe I let her talk me into that shit," Jake grumbles.

"We're going to suck it up," Austin says, his voice stern. "It's for a good cause and we owe Zoey after all the shit she's done for the hockey team when we come in."

It's for a very good cause. The Children's Miracle Center. A place that Zoey holds close to her heart because of her little sister, Chrissy, who has cerebral palsy.

"Well, I know Zoey really appreciates it, and I have no doubt you guys will raise a lot of money with your handsome faces," I add, hoping to stroke their ego and ease the blow.

"Are you going to be there with all of your hot friends to bid on us?" Cam asks, waggling his eyebrows.

"I'll be there. I'm actually helping Zoey set up tomorrow night."

"Us, too. Austin graciously volunteered us without asking, but I don't mind. Zoey's hot and offered to throw in free beer, so it's a win-win."

I bite back a smile when Austin shoots him a pointed look. Before anyone can say more, an alarm pierces through the air, scaring the heck out of me. Everyone's chairs fly out from under them as they jump to their feet and disappear out of the room with lightning speed.

"See ya later, Sam. Thanks for the cookies," Cam yells from down the hall.

I stick my head out and yell back after them. "Be careful!"

It isn't long before I hear the low rumble of fire trucks leaving, their horns and sirens blaring. Staring around the now empty kitchen, I clean up all the coffee mugs and wipe things down before making my own exit.

I'm searching in my purse for my keys as I step out into the warm afternoon sun and crash right into a brick wall. A startled gasp escapes me as I push against that said wall, noticing how slick and sweaty it feels.

"Shit!" Strong arms come around me before I career over, then suddenly I'm staring up into those mesmerizing brown eyes I haven't been able to stop thinking about.

"Hi," I whisper like an idiot, the simple greeting sounding breathless even to my own ears. "I'm sorry. I didn't see you."

"It's fine." He makes no effort to release me. Instead he keeps me close and stares down at me, his gaze focusing on my mouth.

Unintentionally, my tongue darts out to wet my lips as I become rather parched. A noise erupts from him, one I feel vibrate from deep within his chest. His very bare chest that is burning me from the inside out at the moment.

Oh god, why isn't he wearing a shirt? And why does it feel so good to be against his hot skin? Every part of my body tingles with life, especially the one between my legs.

He takes a step back, pulling me from my trance. My small reprieve is short lived when I get a full look at him. Sweat dampens his bronzed skin, reflecting the afternoon sun. Wearing Nike running shoes and loose black gym shorts, it's clear he's out for a run. The shorts hang perfectly on his trim waist, showcasing his impressive V and six-pack.

Wait, no…make that an eight-pack.

Sweet lord.

It should be illegal for him to not wear a shirt outside. With all his bronzed skin and lean muscles on display he's bound to cause an accident.

He stares back at me with a smug grin, amused by my obvious gawking. Heat invades my body again but for a whole other reason.

Shit, not cool. Get a hold of yourself, Sam.

"No one is here. They just got a call," I tell him lamely, breaking the awkward silence.

"I know. I passed them on my way over. What I want to know is what you are doing here, Sam?" By his tone, I can't tell if he's irritated or if he's really just curious.

"My kids and I baked cookies and made a card for you guys to say thank you for having us the other day." When he remains silent, my eyes narrow in annoyance. *"You're welcome."*

My sarcasm earns me a smirk that used to make me want to punch him in the face but now makes my heart skip a beat.

Shaking my head, I move on. "Listen, I'm glad I ran into you...no pun intended," I add, thinking how literal that statement is. "I wanted to tell you I contacted your friend at the department."

"You did?" It's clear he didn't expect me to, and I don't blame him.

"Yeah, and you were right. He's really great. Actually, I um..." I trail off, my eyes dropping to the ground as I begin to feel nervous for some reason. Probably because shame still burns inside of me, hating he knows just how volatile things were with Grant and me.

He slips a finger under my chin and tilts my face back up to his. "You what?"

"I didn't press charges against Grant, but I reported what he did to me and put a restraining order on him," I whisper.

He holds my gaze, something shifting in his eyes, something that looks like pride. "Are you glad you did it?"

I nod. "I am. The only reason I didn't do it sooner is because the last time I did the officer turned out to be friends with him and...it didn't end well for me."

His jaw hardens, fury raging in his dark eyes.

I quickly tread on, not wanting to dwell on Grant anymore. It's humiliating, and a time I want to forget. "Anyway, I just wanted to say thank you for not only giving me your friend's number but for stepping in that night to help me."

He shrugs as if it's no big deal. "I did what anyone else would have done."

"No. Not anyone." I think about how many people in my life turned a blind eye to what was happening, like Grant's friends and colleagues. None as noble as the man standing in front of me. "People like Jake, Cam, and Austin, they would have," I tell him. "My brother, too."

He tenses at the mention of Sawyer.

"As much as you will hate to hear this, Crawford. I've come to learn that you and my brother might have more in common than your big egos."

Rather than elaborating further on that, I sidestep him and leave, not wanting to hear whatever nasty thing will leave his mouth. I love my brother too much to listen to it and well...I'm starting not to hate Jase Crawford all that much either.

CHAPTER 6

Jase

She wasn't supposed to be here but I guess I shouldn't be surprised considering she and Zoey are good friends. She strolled in here tonight, looking like a walking wet dream in her sensible soft blue and white polka dot sundress with her peach fucking scent and peach colored lips, tempting me with things I can't have. Things I shouldn't want.

Who the hell dresses like that to decorate anyway?

Classy women like Samantha Evans, that's who. Trying not to think about her the past few days has proved impossible. Usually I can go months without running into her but now it's like every time I turn around or close my damn eyes, she's right there.

Her gaze had locked with mine before anyone else's and she even gave me a friendly greeting that I barely acknowledged because I'm an asshole. By the way her eyes dimmed it's clear the snub not only caught her off guard but also hurt her.

It made me feel like shit but I shoved aside my guilt, knowing it's what's best for the both of us. We don't like each other that's the way it's always been, it's what I'm familiar with. I don't know what to do with all of these other feelings she drags out of me. I'm especially confused by the need to fuck her like I hate her but then wrap her in my arms and never let anyone hurt her.

I've always been attracted to her, any red-blooded male would be but I'm attracted to a lot of chicks. I'll admit none of them look quite like her, but so what? I can have anyone I want, so why the hell does she mess with my head so bad? If I'm being honest, she always has. There's always been something about her that's drawn me in. I swear it's that damn peach scent of hers. It's fucking addicting.

I shake my head, wanting to punch myself for my crazy ass thoughts. I need to get laid, that's my problem. It's been too long. Longer than usual for me. I need to fuck her out of my head.

Her laughter draws my attention over to the stage where she stands on a stepstool, hanging decorations. Cam's next to her, shaking the stool, being there to catch her when she falls.

Asshole.

"I tell you what, little Evans. You bid on me and I'll take you on a kickass date," he tells her.

I swear I've never been so close to knocking out one of my best friends. By the smirk he tosses over at me, it's clear his intention is to piss me off.

Jake grunts. "Yeah, right. After Evans flies all the way down here to kick your ass."

"I'm not worried, I can take him. Besides, he's due back for a visit anyway."

Sam giggles, shaking her head.

"At least tell me you'll save me if I get a crazy clinger on my hands."

She nods. "I will, but I'm sure you'll be just fine. Girls will be tripping over themselves for you guys."

"I am pretty irresistible."

Another giggle escapes her, the soft melody filling the air and doing shit to my chest that I don't want to feel. As if sensing the weight of my stare, her eyes find mine.

Looking away, I drop down and move back under the table I'm fixing. My wrench is clutched tightly in my fist as I consider beating the shit out of Cam with it. A few minutes later, as I'm tightening the bolts harder than necessary, a pair of long smooth legs come into view next to me along with the aroma of peaches.

"I'm supposed to ask you for a flat head," she says blandly.

Of course Cam sent her over here.

Reaching into the toolbox next to me, I grab the screwdriver and hand it to her without making eye contact.

She takes it from me but makes no move to leave, her sexy legs remaining in my view. "So, we're back to this, Jase?"

"I don't know what you're talking about."

"No? It seems to me like you have a problem that I'm here tonight."

"Doesn't bother me either way." We both know I'm a lying bastard. I do care, way too much. That's the problem.

A frustrated sound leaves her. "You know what? Fine. You want to play this game, then we'll play."

If she only knew how badly I wanted to play with her. The things I would do to that sweet body of hers…

My thoughts trail off when she storms away. I get back to work, hurrying my task so I can get the fuck out of here. As the night wears on, my patience becomes nonexistent. Sam's giggling is constant, Cam doing everything in his power to cause it.

Once I finish setting up the extra tables, I forgo asking Zoey what else she needs and decide now is a good time to leave. If I don't, I'm bound to get into a fight. I toss the tools into the metal box harder than necessary, the loud clanging noise bringing everyone's attention to me.

"I'm out," I announce, but only look at Zoey. "I'll see you tomorrow night."

After she gives me a nod and her thanks, I head for the door.

"Wait, you're leaving, man?" Cam calls out. "Aren't you going to stay and have a beer?"

Turning back, I find Sam standing right next to him. "Nah, I've had about all I can take for tonight."

Ignoring the angry flash of pain in her eyes, I continue on, swinging the door open with enough force to almost rip it off its hinges. The late night air does nothing to calm the inferno raging inside of me. Just as I turn the corner to where I'm parked, I hear the sound of fast clicking heels.

"Jase, wait!" Sam catches up to me at my truck. It's only when I feel her slender fingers grip my arm that I turn back to her. "What the hell is your problem?" she asks, her eyes flashing fire. It matches the one I have roaring in my veins.

"You want to know what my problem is, Sam?"

"Yes, I do. Maybe if you get it off your chest you can stop being such a dick!"

"Fine. I'll tell you." I make the mistake of stepping closer to her, her sweet smell overriding my common sense. "I don't like fucking peaches, okay? I've never liked them. I don't like the smell of them, and I don't like the taste of them. Actually, I hate everything in the peach fucking family. So stop trying to get me to like fucking peaches!"

She stares at me like the lunatic I am, her sparkling green eyes wide and confused. "What the hell does this have to do with peaches?" Shaking her head, she holds up a hand. "You know what? Never mind. I don't care. Know why?" She doesn't wait for a response, her finger jamming into my chest. "Because I hate assholes—I hate everyone in the *asshole family*. So take that and shove it up your peach hatin' ass." She turns to walk away, causing that panic to infiltrate my chest.

"Fuck it." Snagging her wrist, I jerk her against me and claim her mouth the same way I want her body. I swallow her gasp, her peach taste rushing through my system like the sweetest drug.

She's stunned for only a second before her fingers spear into my hair, gripping the strands tight as her tongue duels with mine in a fevered pitch of give and take.

Growling, I lift her off her feet and pin her against my truck. "I lied," I mumble against her lips. "I fucking love peaches. I love the smell of them and goddamn, I love the taste of them."

"Jase," my name falls from her lips on a needy whimper.

I slip my hands under her dress, meeting the bare round globes of her ass and thrust my aching cock against the apex of her thighs.

"Oh god, please!"

Her plea is my undoing. Holding her in place with my hips, I reach for the handle of my back door. The moment it opens I stumble inside, our mouths never severing as I manage to close the door in our tangled haste. Within seconds I have her on her back, my hips cradled between her parted legs.

"Take this off," she breathes, reaching for my shirt, her hands as urgent as mine.

Forgetting where I am, I sit up and nail my head on the fucking roof. "Shit!"

"Oh, are you okay?" she asks, her voice breathless but there's no denying the hint of amusement.

"I will be once my cock is buried inside of you."

A laugh flees her but it trails into a heated moan when I shove my hand up her dress and cup her lace-covered pussy.

"Something funny, Sam?"

"Nope, nothing," she pants. "There's nothing funny about what's happening right now."

She's got that right.

When she reaches for my shirt again, I lean over more, letting her be the one to pull it over my head. Her greedy hands roam over every inch of my exposed flesh. "God, Crawford, I hate admitting this, but you sure do have a great body."

I chuckle at her honesty, knowing how much it probably kills her to say it. "Well, if it makes you feel better, baby, I have no problem telling you how fucking perfect yours is."

"You've never even seen it," she says, amused.

"Trust me, it's hard not to notice." I reach for the straps of her dress but the awkward angle we're in makes it impossible. A growl of frustration works its way up my throat. "There isn't enough fucking room in here for what I want to do to you."

Curving an arm under her waist, I lift her so she's straddling me, our mouths aligning again. She grinds down on me with a moan, begging for what I know will destroy us both, but I'm going to give it to her anyway and it's going to be the best fucking thing I ever do in this lifetime.

I make quick work of her clothes, bunching her dress at her waist as I trail my lips down the slender column of her throat, nipping and sucking hard enough to brand her. I'm going to leave my mark on her because I sure as hell know she's about to leave hers on me.

She already has.

When I reach the swells of her breasts, I pull back to get a look and groan at the sight of her firm perky tits covered in a motherfuckin' peach bra.

I swear, this chick is going to be the death of me.

"You gotta tell me, baby. What the hell is it with you and the color peach?" I ask the question against her lips, once again locked in a heated kiss with her.

I can't seem to stop. I fear I'll never stop. She tastes too fucking good.

"I like coral," she explains, breathing all that peachiness into me. "I don't understand why it's a problem for you."

"It's not," I lie.

It is a problem. A big one that is constantly making my dick hard.

"Just stop talking, Crawford. You're so much hotter when you don't."

A chuckle rumbles from my chest but quickly trails into a groan. "That sassy mouth of yours, baby, is going to get you into trouble one day."

Whatever she's about to say is cut off when I remove her bra and cup the soft weight of her tits, her supple flesh filling my large hands. She arches into my touch, a harsh whimper purging past her lips.

"Jesus, Sam, you're fucking pretty," I growl. Leaning in, I suck a hard pink bud into my mouth, my tongue lashing the fiery tip.

"Oh god!" She falls against the seat behind her, her back bowing further while slender fingers pull my hair. The sting only fuels the need pounding in my veins, shattering the last of my resolve.

Our hands move at the same time—mine shoving under her dress while hers move to my belt. I tear the silk straps of her thong then help her with my pants. The moment I thrust up she drives down, sheathing me into the tightest pussy I've ever felt.

Without a fucking doubt, I know my life has just changed forever.

Fire races through my blood—searing me in places I never knew existed.

"God, Jase. Is this real?" she moans, obviously feeling the same thing I am.

"Yeah, baby. I don't think it gets much more fucking real than this."

I remain still, my eyes closing while I give her time to adjust. It takes every ounce of restraint I possess not to pound into her like an animal.

She's the one who moves first, her hips rocking back and forth.

"That's it. Ride me, baby. Show me how much you want it." My hands cup her firm ass, encouraging every glide.

"It's so good," she moans, her pussy sucking me further into its hot depth.

"So fucking good," I growl. "Tell me you've thought about this as much as I have. That you've thought about my cock filling this tight little pussy of yours."

"Yes, more than I care to admit."

Her truthful answer has me smirking. "When you thought about it, was I fucking you hard or slow?"

"Hard," she pants breathlessly. "Hard and fast."

I freeze, something dark and rich rising to the surface. "Is that what you want, Sam? For me to fuck you hard?"

Her teeth sink into her bottom lip before she gives me a nod. "For one night I want to feel this. Let's get it out of our systems now before it destroys us both."

I have a feeling I'll never get her out of my system, but I'm going to damn well try. For both of our sakes.

My lips move to the soft, warm surface of her shoulder, giving her one more act of tenderness before driving up into her. Unleashing all of the pent-up need I've had for her the past few weeks.

No, years.

For years I've imagined what it would be like to have her and it's better than anything I've ever imagined.

Her screams of pleasure fill the confined space between us as she claws at my shoulders, her nails raking so deep I swear she's drawing blood.

It only fuels me—challenges me.

I want her to scar me so every time I look in the mirror I'll be reminded of this night—of her.

"Oh god, Jase," she whimpers, her pussy fluttering around me with her impending orgasm. "I'm going to come."

"Give it to me, baby. Let me feel it all over my cock." Reaching between us, I slip my finger into her slick heat, finding the swollen bundle of nerves and it sends her flying.

I watch her shatter above me. Her hair a tangled mess around her face, her cheeks tinged pink and sexy peach colored lips parted in ecstasy.

She's the hottest goddamn thing I've ever seen and I make sure to commit it all to memory before allowing myself to follow after her. A groan shreds from my throat as I'm thrown into an abyss of fiery pleasure.

She falls against me, our sweat-dampened skin melding together as we try to catch our breaths. My hand buries into the back of her long blonde hair when she turns her face into the crook of my neck.

"What just happened?" she asks through labored breaths, sounding as confused as I feel.

My response is a kiss to her temple because I don't have an answer for her. I have no words for what just happened. But I have a very strong feeling that I will be dreaming of fucking peaches for the rest of my life.

CHAPTER 7

Sam

I'm a traitor and a whore. I'm a traitorous whore who fucked her brother's enemy in the back of his truck like a floozy. And I liked it.

No—I loved it!

Oh god. How did it happen? My head is still reeling from it. One minute I was charging after him, ready to give him a piece of my mind for being such a jerk, then the next instant we were ripping each other's clothes off like sex-starved animals. He devoured me in a way I've only ever dreamed about. It's something I will never forget as long as I live. What happened between us was more than anything I've ever experienced.

It makes no sense.

We were so caught up in the moment we didn't even use a condom. I have never done that before. I'm too sensible for that but, with him, he completely overrides my common sense.

We spoke about it after, when reality began to sink in. Thankfully, I'm on the pill and he assured me he was clean, that they are tested regularly at the fire department. He also told me that he's always used one before. I believe him, and I get a sick satisfaction knowing I got a part of him no one else ever has.

God, what is wrong with me?

I feel like I betrayed my brother, or my whole family for that matter, considering Jase doesn't seem to like any of them. Including me. But he sure seemed to like me last night. The subtle ache between my thighs and the mark on my neck that I'm hiding with my hair is a beautiful reminder.

We had silently lain in his truck long after the fact, his arms holding me close while we both tried to come to grips with what we did. I expected him to want me to leave right after. Wham, bam, thank you, ma'am, but it wasn't like that at all. I think both of us would have stayed all night in that spot if we could have but we knew we couldn't.

After he drove me home he left me with a kiss I'll remember forever. It wasn't like any of the kisses we had shared earlier in the evening. It was slow—soft—meaningful. It was the most beautiful kiss I've ever had.

It destroyed all other kisses up to this point and probably will shatter every other one to come.

Now here I am, twenty-four hours later, back at Overtime, seated at one of the small tables that are amongst tons of women. A paddle is in my hand, ready to bid for a good cause. But all I can think about is the man that ruined me for anyone else in one damn night.

I need to pull my head out of the Jase clouds it's in and move on. It was one night. A night that he probably has already forgotten… Just the thought has lead settling in the pit of my stomach.

"So are you ready for this or what?" Zoey asks with an excited smile as she takes the seat across from me, having no idea of my inner turmoil.

"I'm ready," I say, raising my paddle and also my gin and tonic, taking a hefty sip since I'm going to need it. A lot of it. I know why she's excited though, this is a big night that could potentially raise a lot of money to help the Miracle Center her sister is in.

"I have a check for you from my father," I tell her.

She gives me an appreciative yet sad smile. "He didn't have to do that."

"He wanted to. You know he would give far more if you would accept it."

"Your family has already gone above and beyond for Chrissy and me. I'm indebted to them for life."

I'm about to tell her she owes us nothing but I'll just sound like a broken record. Instead, I reach over and take her hand, giving it a gentle squeeze.

Her eyes are suddenly drawn to something behind me and she groans. "I guess I shouldn't be surprised."

"What?"

She lifts her chin for me to look. I turn in my seat, my blood heating at the sight of Stephanie.

Great!

I bet I know whom she plans to bid for...the thought has jealousy heating my blood.

She spots us right away, her nose lifting as she makes her way over to us. Or rather, toward me since her eyes are locked with mine.

"Samantha," she says, in that snotty tone of hers.

"Stephanie," I mock back.

"Decided to leave the playground?"

Zoey stands, ready to come to my defense, but I ward her off with a lift of my hand. "Actually, I did. I came to support a good cause."

"And just who are you bidding for?" she asks. When I remain silent, refusing to play her game, she leans into my personal space, her eyes narrowing. "Let's make one thing clear. Jase is mine, so back off."

I tense, wondering why she'd think I'd be here for him.

"I'm not stupid," she says, sensing my thoughts. "It's obvious to everyone. Stay away from him."

It's on the tip of my tongue to tell her she can have him but it would be a lie. I might not be able to have him but I most certainly will not be giving him to her on a silver platter.

"I'll bid on whoever I want," I tell her. "Whether it be Jase or any of the other guys."

"We'll see about that." She starts away but Zoey grabs her arm before she can make it far.

"Cause any problems, Stephanie, and not only will I have you thrown out but you will never be allowed back in here again. Tonight is important. Don't ruin it."

She rips her arm out of Zoey's grasp, her chin jutting out. "I'm here to support a good cause like everyone else."

Yeah right, the only cause she'll be supporting is the one that requires her to get on her knees.

"Good. Keep it that way," Zoey says.

Turning her nose back up, Stephanie walks away, thankfully to a table at the other end of the room.

"God, I can't stand her!" I grit out.

"I know. None of us can, but her money is as good as anyone else's. For that reason alone I can put up with her for a few hours." She takes her seat again, her eyes pinning me in place. "So, are you ever going to fill me in on what happened when you stormed out after Jase last night and never came back?"

My eyes dart away from hers as I take another gulp of my drink. "Yep, one day. Just not tonight."

I haven't come to terms with it myself yet so there's no way I'd be able to explain my actions to anyone else.

She chuckles, shaking her head. "I already know, but I can't wait for the juicy details."

Oh, they're juicy all right.

Thankfully, I'm saved from having to say more when a woman in a dress suit takes the stage. "Good evening, ladies, and thank you for joining us tonight for our first annual Date For A Cause auction. My name is Lindy Armstrong, president of the fundraising committee at the Children's Miracle Center, and I will be your MC for the night. I want to send out a special thank you to Zoey Anderson for not only coming up with this magnificent idea but for allowing us to host it here in her establishment. The turnout has been more than we could have hoped for."

As we all applaud Zoey gives a shy smile and a short wave, uncomfortable with the attention.

"Who here is ready to meet our fine gentlemen of the hour?"

I smile at the next round of applause and can't help but feel sorry for all the guys. Well, except for Cam. He'll eat this up, but I'm sure the rest of them will feel awkward about a bunch of women bidding for their time. Or maybe not.

Will Jase be? Or will he soak it up like Cam?

It doesn't matter, Sam. Don't think about him. Bid on someone else, it will be a good distraction.

"Without further ado, please welcome the charming and courageous men of Fire Station Two."

The entire place erupts in applause, women whistling and catcalling as sixteen spiffed up men in black tuxedos walk out and line up. My eyes immediately stray to the one man I haven't stopped thinking about. The one whose touch I can still feel burning beneath my skin.

All the memories of last night come flooding back on a rush, making my entire body flush with heat. His eyes move along the crowd, as if he's searching for someone. It's not long before they lock with mine. The entire place fades away as we stare at one another. There's no exchange, not a wave or a smile, but there's no denying the electricity that passes between us. It's powerful enough to pin me in place.

"Good god they're beautiful," Zoey says, breaking through the spell that had been cast upon me. "What the hell is it about a tuxedo that makes an ordinary man look...extraordinary?"

I'm a girl who appreciates the simplicity of a pair of kick ass jeans and a T-shirt but there is no denying the way these men fill out a suit, especially Jase. But I have a feeling there isn't much out there that wouldn't make him look good.

After Lindy goes through the rules and explains how it will work she introduces the first guy, Tristan, who I've never met but have seen around. She starts the bidding at seventy-five dollars and he has no problem being bid on. It ends up tapping out at five hundred dollars.

A great start.

The next three are close to the same. When Cam is called up, his bid finishes at twelve hundred dollars.

"Oh my god, this is insane," Zoey says excitedly. "I knew it would be a hit."

Austin is called up next, dozens of paddles rising once again, including Zoey's.

"I don't think so, ladies. This one's mine," she says, chasing each bid.

"You have a thing for Austin?" I ask, shock coursing through me.

She shrugs. "Of course. Who wouldn't? If I had the time I'd have already snatched him up, but as you know, I don't."

That's because the responsibility of her sister lies solely on her since their mother is a deadbeat.

"But I can spare one night and that one is going to be with him."

Nothing would make me happier if she and Austin hooked up, because I know he would treat her the way she deserves. Zoey is used to having to take care of everyone. It would be nice to see it happen to her for a change but it would be a tough wall to knock down. She's stubborn.

I applaud loudly when she wins the bid, paying a thousand dollars. However, my excitement dies when Jase is called up next. I consider locking myself in the bathroom until this is over so I won't give into temptation.

My stomach clenches at all the paddles being lifted, Stephanie, of course, being in the lead, constantly raising each bid. It takes every ounce of self-control I have not to jump in.

Thankfully, one lady continues to raise her, and as much as I hate to see Jase on a date with someone, I'll take anyone over her. Unfortunately, the lady drops out at eleven hundred dollars.

"Eleven hundred," Lindy announces. "Do I hear twelve?"

My heart pounds and palms sweat at the blanketed silence. Jealousy spreads through me at the triumphant smile on Stephanie's smug face.

"Eleven hundred going once—twice—"

It's then that my traitorous body has a mind of its own. I jump to my feet with my paddle in the air. "Thirteen!" I yell, feeling my legs quake beneath me.

"Yes!" Zoey hisses.

My eyes lock with Jase's and I'm not sure who is more surprised—me or him.

"Thirteen." Lindy points at me excitedly. "The highest bid so far tonight. Do I hear fourteen?"

"Fourteen!" Stephanie tosses out, her anger evident.

"Fifteen!"

"Eighteen!" she yells, throwing a challenging look my way.

"Get her, Sam. I have some room on my credit card!" Zoey grinds out.

I would never take Zoey's money but I raise her anyway, knowing I will figure out some way to get it. Even if I have to ask my father. Yeah, that would go over really well. I can just see it now. *"Hey, Dad, I know you hate Jase Crawford and all but can you loan me a few thousand bucks. I sorta paid to have a date with him."*

Oh god, I'm pathetic…but not enough to stop.

It turns into a battle. Our paddles lifting after one another. The higher it rises, the faster my adrenaline rushes.

Jase shakes his head at me, telling me to bow out. I don't know if it's because he wants to go on a date with her or he doesn't want me spending that much. I'm hoping it's the latter because I can't stop. I can't let her win. It will totally kill my pride and well…probably my heart.

When we get to twenty five hundred dollars I can't take it anymore and jump ahead, hoping to end this once and for all. "Four thousand dollars!"

Gasps sound around the room just before it falls to a dead silence, everyone freezing in place.

Oh shit!

"What the hell are you doing?" Jase gapes at me from the stage, his words loud enough to hear.

"Amazing," Lindy says, sounding as shocked as I feel. "Four thousand going once, twice… Sold!"

The knot in my stomach tightens.

What did I just do?

Stephanie wastes no time approaching me. Her expression is stoic but her eyes are raging. I brace myself for the catfight I'm sure is about to ensue.

"Only you would have to pay that much to get a date. I, on the other hand, already had him for free," she taunts, giving me a smug smile.

Before I can tell her to go to hell she's gone, leaving me to stand here like an idiot.

"Ignore her, Sam. She's jealous," Zoey says, trying to make me feel better.

I look around the place, the next bid already off and running. My eyes land on Jase again to find him still staring at me like I've lost my mind.

Shaking my head, I swipe my purse from the table. "I'm sorry, I have to go. I'll call you later."

I feel bad ignoring Zoey when she calls me back, but I need to get out of here before I completely lose it. Pushing through the door, I step out into the fresh air, the cool evening breeze a welcome relief to the fire invading my cheeks.

Jase comes crashing out not long after me. Unable to deal with him right now, I turn away and move for my car.

"I don't think so, baby." He grabs my arm and swings me around to face him. "What the hell was that? Are you fucking crazy?"

I rip my arm back, all my pent-up anger bubbling up to the surface and exploding like dynamite. "Yes, I am! I'm crazy because she makes me *crazy* and so do you. Now I'm standing here in the parking lot screaming like a crazy person, but you know what? I don't give a shit," I yell, unable to stop my tirade, no matter how much my mind is telling me to shut up. "Everyone always talks about how sensible Sam is. Well Sensible Sam has finally lost it. First I fuck my brother's enemy in the back of his truck, then spend four thousand dollars on a date with him, but at least that one is for a good cause. So you all can take Sensible Sam and shove her up your asses!" By the time I finish, my throat is dry and chest heaving.

Jase stares back at me, seeming at a loss for words, the beginning of a smile playing at the edge of his perfect lips.

Releasing a deflated breath, I drop back against the concrete building. "I really have lost my damn mind," I mumble.

With a chuckle he falls back next to me. "Well, we're all bound to lose it sooner or later. I lost it over peaches last night," he says, tossing a sexy smirk my way.

"I just couldn't do it," I admit on a whisper. "I couldn't let her win. Usually, I'm not catty, but she brings out the worst in me."

He grunts. "Yeah, she's got a gift for that."

Glancing over at him, I gather up the courage to ask a question I fear to know the answer to. "Are you upset I spent that kind of money or because you wanted that date with her?"

His eyes narrow. "What the hell do you think?"

I shrug. "I have no idea. That's why I'm asking you. She seems to think you guys have more. Regardless of the money I spent, I have more pride than to be someone's second choice."

I'm caught off guard when he pushes from the wall and crowds me against it, his arms caging me in on either side of my head. "Let's get a few things straight. Stephanie and I have been over for years. It ended the night she fucked your brother and it has stayed that way."

It's on the tip of my tongue to defend Sawyer, but I don't get the chance.

"Secondly," he says, his hand moving to brush my hair away from my neck where it hides the mark he left on me. My pulse speeds up as his thumb caresses it. "You could never be someone's second choice, Sam. You're too good for that."

He's wrong. I've been people's second choice. I was Grant's second choice many times when it came to other women. I was such a fool back then.

"Do you have that kind of money?" he asks, changing the subject.

"Yeah," I lie. I'll find a way to come up with it. I would never back out.

"Then I guess I owe you a date," he says, sending butterflies to dance in my tummy.

I try to mask the effect by crossing my arms over my chest. "For four thousand dollars it better be a good one, Crawford."

With a smirk he snags me around the waist and pulls me flush against his hard body. "Trust me, baby. It'll be worth every fucking penny." His warm brown eyes hold me captive as his mouth descends upon mine, stealing my breath and crashing into my soul like a freight train.

How on earth does he do that?

Uncaring at the moment, I wrap my arms around his neck and take what I haven't stopped thinking about since last night.

Growling, his tongue glides in, doing an erotic dance with mine that sends my heart and senses reeling. We stay locked in the heated bliss for so long I lose track of time along with oxygen, but I couldn't care less. I don't care if I ever breathe again if he's the one stealing it from me.

With his fingers gently gripping either side of my jaw, he pulls back, but remains close, his lips hovering just above mine.

Slowly, I open my eyes and find him staring down at me, his intense gaze penetrating the depths of my soul.

"I'll pick you up next Saturday at four. Be ready."

My gaze narrows, his order cutting through my lust-induced haze. Just when I'm about to say something he steals my lips one more time with a quick, hard kiss then starts off to his truck.

"Hey! How do you know I'm free? Maybe I already have plans," I yell, feeling my blood heat at his audacity.

His hand rests on the handle of his truck when he turns back to me, gracing me with that sexy yet irritating smirk of his. "If you do then cancel them," he says so casually. "For that entire night and following morning, Sam—you're mine."

Without another word, he climbs into his truck and drives away, leaving me to gape after him.

He has some nerve!

We'll see how smooth he is when he shows up at my apartment and I'm not there… Oh, who the hell am I kidding. I'll be there waiting, anticipating what I'm sure will be another unforgettable night with him.

I'm in so much trouble.

CHAPTER 8

Jase

A few days later, I walk into my childhood home, my stomach immediately grumbling from the sweet smell of baking.

Ah, a perfect day to stop by.

Walking into the kitchen, I find my mom pulling out squares, muffins, and banana loaf from the oven. She turns around when my boots hit the linoleum, a genuine smile spreading across her face.

"Jasiah," she says, using my full name. "I didn't know you were stopping by today." Losing her oven mitts, she comes over and pulls me down to kiss the shit out of my face.

"Hey, Mom," I grumble, thankful no one else is here to witness this shit. I would never say anything to her about it though because I know it would hurt her feelings. And no one hurts my mom's feelings, not without the wrath of my father or me.

She takes my face between her hands and looks me over. "I swear you get more handsome every time I see you. Just like your father," she says. "When are you gonna give me grandbabies?"

I grunt but refuse to answer. It will turn into a long, drawn-out conversation like always, and I don't have time for that today.

Thankfully, she gets the message. "Okay, I'll leave you alone." Smiling, she gives a hard pat to my cheek. "I'm glad you came by. You must have a sixth sense. I'm baking for you and your friends at the station," she says, turning back to her pans on the stove.

She's crazy if she thinks I'm sharing any of that with the guys. I'm keeping it all for myself. They have their own moms to bake for them.

"Have a seat, honey. You want something to drink?" she asks, coming to place a warm chocolate chip muffin down in front of me.

"I'm good, thanks though."

"Let me call for your father. He's tinkering away in the garage again." She walks over to the kitchen window above the sink and slides it open. "Ben! Come inside, Jasiah is here."

I wince at how loud she is, wishing for just once she would relent and call me Jase.

My dad comes in the back door a minute later, wiping his hands with a grease-stained towel. He takes my mother in his arms, dips her, and lays a long, drawn-out kiss on her before making his way over to me.

"Hey, my boy, how're you doing?" he asks, pulling me to stand and wrapping me in a quick, firm hug.

"Hey, Dad. I'm good."

"What brings you by? Did you smell your mom's baking all the way across town?" he asks with a chuckle, taking a seat at the table.

"Nope, but clearly it was a good day to pop in."

"Every day is a good day for you to visit," my mom adds, giving me a pointed look.

"Come on, Mom, it hasn't been that long."

"It's been almost a month." She holds up a hand to ward off my protest. "I know. It's not that long in the grand scheme of things but it is when you live so close. You know I'd give anything to see your handsome face every day if I could."

If she had her way, I'd still be living at home.

"Well, look on the bright side, at least you get to see this handsome one every day," I say, gesturing over to my dad.

"Damn straight, and you don't get much better than mine."

We both chuckle at the way my mom rolls her eyes but she can't hide her smile. "Well, I guess I can't argue that," she agrees, giving my dad a few gentle pats on the cheek. "Anyway, how did that fundraiser go this weekend?"

"It was…interesting." Actually, it was fucking awkward as hell. Until the end of the night when I got to taste Sam again. "It sounds like a lot of money was raised," I add.

"That's wonderful. Does that mean you have a date?" she asks hopefully, an almost gleeful smile taking over her face.

It's because I don't date…at least not conventionally, but Sam is a different story. She's worth a date.

She's worth much more.

"Yep. Actually, that's why I'm here." I look at my dad. "Do you still have the route mapped out when we went camping in the mountains a few years back?"

He nods. "You bet. It's in my desk drawer."

"You're taking her camping in the mountains?" my mom asks, sounding unsure.

"No," I answer, but offer nothing more.

"All right, fine, be cryptic but will you at least tell me her name? Do I know her?"

"Yeah, you know of her…" I trail off, unsure of how to tell them who it is.

"Oh, Jase, don't tell me it's Stephanie," she says, disdain sharpening her words.

I grunt. "Thankfully no, but it was close. It came down to her and one other bidder by the end."

"Oh, thank goodness for that. That girl is no good. She never has been."

She's a bitch and a mistake I will always regret.

"So, who is it?" my dad asks.

"Samantha Evans."

"Really?" my mom asks, her eyes widening in shock.

I nod.

"Wait, Samantha Evans as in John Evans's daughter?" he asks, not seeming all that thrilled about it, which I expected.

"Yep, the same one."

"Boy," he starts in on me. "You be careful. I hold no grudge against that girl. I don't even know her, but that father of hers is an asshole."

"Listen, Dad. I get it. I do. Her brother is an asshole too, but this date has nothing to do with either of them and she's not like that. She's cool."

She's much more than cool but I keep that to myself.

"Well I've spoken with Catherine a few times and she has always been lovely so I'm sure her daughter is the same way."

My dad grunts. "The problem in that family isn't with the women. It's the men."

I agree with him, although I don't know John Evans well but her brother is a different story, and he had to learn about being a jackass from somewhere.

"Whatever happened between you guys?" I ask him.

He shrugs. "Nothing happened per se," he starts. "The guy is just an arrogant son of a bitch. Thinks his shit don't stink and no one is as good as his precious son."

"Sounds like someone else I know," my mom mumbles.

"The hell it does," my father shoots back, getting all worked up. "We might not have a problem admitting when we're good at some-thing"—he gestures between the two of us—"but we aren't assholes about it."

Exactly! There's a difference between confidence and arrogance.

"Whatever you say," she sighs before pointing a finger at me. "Ei-ther way, I raised you right, Jasiah. I want you to prove it. You treat her good—respect her. She's not a conquest. Bring her flowers and show her a nice time."

"Don't worry, Mom. I got this."

I might not date but I always respect the chicks I'm with. It's a mutual arrangement. However, I know Sam is different, and I plan to spend a day and evening with her that both of us will never forget.

CHAPTER 9

Sam

I must have changed my outfit at least a dozen times. All his text said was dress casual and comfortable. He wouldn't give me anything else. Not one hint as to what we're doing. Doesn't he realize how vague that is? Causal and comfortable could mean a variety of things.

Leave it to him to drive me nuts.

Though, I can't deny the butterflies swirling in my tummy. All week I've looked forward to this then berated myself for it. One more time. One more night with him. I just want to feel that connection once more.

To feel…*alive.*

That's the best way to explain it. That night in his truck was reckless and so unlike me but it was the first time I've felt alive in a long time. I have no idea what's in store for us today but I plan to embrace it and enjoy it for what it is.

I finally decided on a pair of cutoff jean shorts that mold to my skin like butter. They are the comfiest ones I own and are very flattering, especially for my backside. I paired it with a flowy army green tank that makes my green eyes more pronounced.

I warm thinking about the new Victoria Secret bra and panties I have on underneath that I bought just for him. That's of course if we get to that point tonight. By his parting comment last weekend, I'm assuming we will. Just the thought has heat gathering between my thighs.

One more time.

The sound of my phone ringing cuts through my thoughts. Grabbing my cell from the nightstand, my heart swells with love at the picture of my sister's face flashing on the screen.

"Well, if it isn't my favorite sister in the whole world," I answer.

"The one and only." The smile I hear in her voice matches the one on my face. "There's a small moment of reprieve in the boutique so I wanted to call and check in. How are things?"

"Good. I'm actually just waiting to be picked up for a date," I say, knowing I shouldn't tell her but need to talk to someone about it.

"A date," she squeals excitedly. "Who is it? Do I know him?" There's a pause, her enthusiasm diminishing. "Don't tell me it's with that two-timing bastard."

"No. I told you, I'm done with Grant."

"Good. Then who is it?"

"Promise you won't tell a soul?"

"Oh my god, I can't tell anyone? This is so damn juicy. Yes, I promise. Now tell me before I die of curiosity."

I laugh, her excitement fueling my own. "Actually, it's …it's Jase Crawford."

There's a long moment of silence, so long that I think she's hung up.

"Jesse? You still there?" I ask nervously.

"You're joking, right?"

I sigh, my excitement deflating. "I know how this looks. It's crazy even to me but—"

"Oh, it's more than crazy. It's downright suicidal. Do you have any idea what Sawyer will do if he finds out?"

"He's not going to find out. It's just one date. No big deal."

"It's a very big deal. This is our brother's enemy, Sam. And let's not forget Dad and Mr. Crawford's little rivalry they've had forever. How did this even come about?"

"Honestly, I'm not sure," I admit, feeling more conflicted by the second. "Oh, Jesse, I'm so confused. I mean, the guy drives me insane.

One minute we're yelling at each other then the next we're tearing each other's clothes off and having sex in the backseat of his truck."

"Holy shit! You slept with him?" The high shrill of her voice has me jerking the phone away from my ear.

"Yeah…"

"My sister—my sweet, innocent, little sister had sex with Jase Crawford in the back of his truck?"

"Yes," I repeat, letting out a soft sigh. "And if I'm being honest, it was one of the most incredible things I've ever experienced."

"Oh, I'll bet. I have no doubt that cocky asshole knows exactly what to do with that dick of his."

We both burst into a fit of laughter, my cheeks heating at the memory, but I sober quickly. "The thing is, Jesse. He's not that much of an asshole. I mean, sometimes yeah, but…he's been good to me. He was there for me one night when I really needed someone."

"What happened?" she asks, concern thick in her voice.

I decide to share a little bit with her. Not all of it. They can never know how bad things were with Grant. "Grant showed up one night at Overtime and was a jerk as usual. Jase put him in his place."

And broke his face.

"That bastard! I wish Sawyer would have done more than break his nose," she seethes, talking about the time Sawyer paid him an unexpected visit.

"I'm just glad Jase was there. Grant wouldn't take a hint but I think he has now."

Considering he had a box shipped to me this week of a few items I had left at his place with most of it broken, I've taken it as a sure sign that he is as done with me as I am him.

"Well, I'm glad he was there for you too, but…"

"What?" I ask when she trails off.

"Are you sure he isn't using you as a way to get back at Sawyer?"

"No," I say, shutting down the suggestion right away.

It can't be. He wouldn't do that, and I know whatever this is between us, he feels it, too.

"It's different than anything I've ever felt, Jesse. I know it's reckless and crazy but...I need that right now. I can't explain it."

"You don't have to. I can hear it in your voice. Something I haven't heard in a long time," she says softly. "Sometimes, crazy and reckless is a good thing. So despite my fear of our brother finding out, I'm telling you take this for all it's worth and enjoy it. Especially if it means finding that Sam we haven't seen in a very long time."

"I'm finding her," I reply on a choked whisper, emotion burning its way up my throat. "She's almost back."

"Good."

A knock on my door breaks up our moment. "Jesse, it's him. I gotta go."

She sighs. "All right. Have fun and promise you will call me tomorrow with all the details."

"Promise."

"I love you, Sammy."

"I love you, too," I whisper. "I'll talk to you tomorrow."

"Bye."

Hanging up, I shake myself of the heavy moment and do a quick check in the mirror, fluffing my hair. Then, with my tummy dancing, I head to the door and take a deep breath before opening it.

Jase stands on the other end, looking sexy as sin in a pair of well-worn jeans that hang just right on him and a black T-shirt that stretches across his broad shoulders. His dark hair that's usually covered with a hat is unruly, yet still looks perfectly in place at the same time. My fingers curl with the urge to feel the soft strands between them again.

His eyes do some traveling of their own, sweeping down me from head to toe. By the way his gaze darkens you would think I was naked instead of wearing a pair of shorts and a tank top.

"Hi," I greet him, trying to break the tension but sound ridiculously breathless.

He flashes me those perfect white teeth of his. "Hi, Peaches...or

Sensible Sam," he says, bringing a smile to my face. "Which one are you today?"

"Just Sam. I'd appreciate it if we kept it that way and not channeled the crazy Sam. Think you can manage that, Crawford?"

With a husky chuckle that does weird things to my insides, he steps in and hooks an arm around my waist before pulling me flush against him. "Yeah, baby, I think I can manage that." Without warning, he claims my mouth in a mind-numbing kiss.

Sighing, I give into the rush of emotions and wrap my arms around his neck, relishing in the warmth that settles all the way down to my bones.

No holding back—not today.

Growling, he kicks the door closed behind him and lifts me off my feet with the arm that's wrapped around me. "It's been a whole week since I tasted this," he says against my lips. "I missed it."

His confession catches me by surprise. "Me, too," I admit, even though I shouldn't.

"We're going to make up for it tonight," he says, placing me back to my feet. "But first…" He hands me the small gift bag he's holding.

"What on earth is this?" I ask, taking the bag from him.

"A gift. I don't date but figured since I'm doing it this once I may as well do it with style," he adds with a wink.

Opening the bag with a smile, I pull out a plain white box and slide it open to reveal a dainty silver bangle bracelet. The single glass peach charm dangling from it has me chuckling. "You have a strange fascination with peaches, Crawford."

"Yeah, it seems I do."

My eyes move to his, finding no amusement there. Instead, I find something else, something deeper that can't be described.

"It's beautiful, thank you," I whisper, surprised and touched that he would buy me something like this.

"My mom told me to bring you flowers but there were no peach colored ones, only orange and that's not good enough. Besides, flowers die anyway," he adds, walking closer to put the bracelet on me. "So when I walked out of the flower shop, I passed by this boutique and low and behold there in the front window was this bracelet...with a single peach charm. Go figure."

"Yeah, go figure," I say, thinking about how some things happen at the perfect moment. "This is the nicest thing anyone has done for me in a really long time, Jase."

"Well, that's sad, Peaches. You deserve things like this every day."

I stare up at him, my heart overflowing. "Sometimes, you're really nice."

"I'm always nice, just ask my mom."

Smiling. I look down at my bracelet, fingering the glass charm. "I really do love it. Thank you."

"You're welcome." Slinging his arm around my neck, he drops a kiss on the top of my head, the simple gesture warming my heart. "Come on, let's get out of here. We have twenty-five minutes to be at our destination. Can't be late."

"Are you finally going to tell me where we're going?"

"Nope but before we leave change your flip flops for running shoes and grab a sweater to bring, just in case."

I do as he says, my interest piquing further. "Is the rest of my outfit okay?" I ask, bending down to tie my shoes.

A low growl penetrates the air. Looking behind me, I catch him staring at my ass. He rubs his clean-shaven jaw... "Yeah, baby. It's fucking perfect."

My stomach tightens at the low husk of his voice.

This is going to be a long afternoon.

On the way to our destination, I plead for some sort of hint but he remains tight-lipped and enjoys every moment of my torture. Thankfully, it isn't long until we arrive at the scenic tour station where you can explore mountain views from a gondola. Jase climbs out of the truck and comes over to let me out.

"You're taking me on a gondola ride, Crawford?" I ask, excited at the prospect. I've lived here my whole life and have never done it.

"Yeah, something like that," he answers cryptically. Grabbing my hand, he leads me to where a man is waiting for us outside the lift. "Jase, it's good to see you," he says, shaking his hand.

"You, too. Thanks for helping me out."

"No problem."

"This is Samantha Evans," Jase says, introducing me. "Sam, this is Glen Perkins. He owns the place."

"It's nice to meet you."

"You, too," he replies, shaking my hand before returning his attention to Jase. "The weather is perfect right now for you."

"It is," Jase agrees with a nod.

Their exchange has me even more curious.

"Bert's waiting up at the top."

"Great. Thanks."

"You bet. Have fun and be safe."

"I'm always safe."

The older man grunts, clearly knowing Jase better than that.

With a chuckle, Jase leads me into the gondola.

"Shouldn't he be coming with us?" I ask, feeling a little anxious as the doors close.

"No." He takes a seat on the bench and looks at me with a frown. "You have been on one of these before, right?"

I shake my head.

"Never?" he asks incredulously.

"Pathetic, huh?"

He graces me with a sexy smirk. "Come here."

When I take his outstretched hand, he pulls me down on his lap, and that's when we begin making our climb. The first jolt catches me off guard and has me tensing.

"Don't be nervous. We're safe," he says, pressing a kiss to my bare shoulder.

I relax against him, finding safety in his strong arms. The view is breathtaking. The afternoon sun bounces off the white caps of the mountains, reflecting off their sharp peaks, displaying what God so graciously created.

"It really is beautiful, isn't it?" I say, finding a new appreciation for what I've always taken for granted.

"Just wait. You haven't seen anything yet."

I turn toward him, my arm curling around his neck. "You come up here often?"

"Yeah. Every chance I get."

"What do you do?"

"You're about to find out," he answers, still refusing to tell me.

"Remember that small pep talk we had about not channeling crazy Sam?"

He chuckles, amused with my frustration. "Keep her locked up, baby. She can come out later tonight and play," he says with a dirty grin.

The sexy bastard.

Once we make it to the top, Jase links his fingers with mine as if it's the most natural thing and walks over to the man who is waiting for us. Tons of equipment circles his feet, one of them a parachute, which has my pulse kick starting.

"Jase!" he greets him with a handshake.

"Hey, Bert, thanks for meeting us up here."

"You bet. Everything is here for you. Just give me a call with your coordinates when you land, and I'll bring you your truck."

Coordinates? Land?

My heart beats double-time, not liking the sound of this. I barely acknowledge the gentlemen's brief greeting to me as he walks away, my eyes glued to all the things on the ground that look like death traps.

Jase drops down on his knee, sorting through the pile, oblivious to my inner turmoil.

"Uh, Jase. Can you tell me now what we're doing?" I ask, noticing how dry my throat is.

He looks up at me, excitement lit all over his handsome face. "We're paragliding."

"We are?"

"Yep," he answers, his attention returning to the scattered equipment.

"On this mountain?"

"Well, technically off the mountain."

I stare at him, wondering if this is a cruel joke. "You want me to jump off this mountain?"

"Not jump, baby. Glide," he explains, as if that makes it better.

"I don't think I can do this."

The small tremble in my voice finally brings his gaze back to mine. Realizing my fear, he stands and moves for me. "Hey, Sam, it's okay," he says, grabbing my shoulders.

"No. It's not. I've never done anything like this before. I don't have the slightest clue what to do."

"It's okay. You don't have to. You're going to be strapped to me."

"Strapped to you?" I repeat slowly.

"Yeah. You don't have to do anything. I do it all and I've done it a million times. I swear, it's safe."

I look behind him, unable to see what's over the ledge and not wanting to either.

Can I really do this? Do I want to? Is Jesse right and he's just trying to get back at Sawyer and his plan is to kill me by making it look like a paragliding accident?

Okay, Sam. Settle down, I berate myself for the ridiculous thought.

His warm hands cradle my face, bringing my gaze back to his, regret reflecting back at me. "I should have thought more about it. I wanted to do this with you because it's probably one of the coolest things you will ever experience, but I should have asked you first. It's not for everyone." His voice is soft and gentle with understanding. "I'll put in a call to Bert and tell him we're coming back down." Brushing a kiss to my lips, he reaches for his phone.

"No, don't. It's okay," I protest, feeling guilty after he went to all this work.

"I'm not going to take you if you're that scared. It's fine; we'll go back down and head to our next spot. I still have other things planned."

"No, really, Jase. I'm all right."

He stares back at me for the liar I am.

"Okay, I'm nervous," I admit. "Like, really nervous, but I don't want that to stop me from doing it, especially when I will probably never get the opportunity again."

He pulls me against him, his body heat melting away the icy fear freezing inside of me. "You sure? Because it's not a big deal for us to go back down."

"I'm sure. Just…promise me you won't crash us."

His lips quirk in amusement. "I promise. You're safe with me. I'd never let anything happen to you."

I believe that with my whole heart. That's why I'm going to do this, even though I'm terrified out of my mind.

"Come on." He leads me over to the equipment and makes me put on my thin hoodie before suiting me up. Starting with the harness and finishing with the helmet. He goes over a few simple instructions with me as he finishes with himself. After spreading out the parachute behind him, he extends his hand to me. "Trust me, Sam."

My heart stalls in my chest, something familiar tugging at the dark recesses of my mind. Shaking myself of the bizarre feeling, I put my hand in his and allow him to drag me in closer. After hooking me up to his harness, he hoists me up. My legs wrap around his waist and arms around his neck, as I cling to him like a koala bear. My nerves begin to settle from the feel of his strong, warm body.

"No passing out on me, Peaches," he jokes, but his voice is gruff, letting me know he feels the same current I am. The same one that always seems to pass between us.

"You need to be more concerned about me puking on you," I grumble.

I'm rewarded with a deep chuckle. "I've been through worse. Just hold on to me and you'll be good." Bending down, he grabs the two black handles then brings us back to full height. "You ready?"

I let out a terrified breath, feeling close to losing my lunch. "No, but I don't think I ever will be."

"I have you, I promise." He backs up a little then starts running like he explained he would do earlier.

My arms tighten around him as we approach the edge, my heart pounding like a jackhammer. I close my eyes; unable to bear watching us go over.

A whoosh of air hits me before I feel the jerk of the parachute catch. I squeal in fear and bury my face into his neck. "Oh my god. Oh my god. Oh my god."

"We're up!" I barely hear him through the blood rushing in my ears. I cling to him even tighter, not daring to move. "Babe, you're choking the shit out of me," he says on a strangled laugh.

"Sorry." I loosen my grip around his neck but tighten my legs on his waist.

"Take a look, Sam."

"That's okay. I'm good."

"Come on. Don't miss out on this."

Releasing a shaky sigh, I summon the courage to lift my head and slowly open my eyes. My breath immediately locks in my throat with a gasp as I take in the sight before me.

Oh my god.

This pales in comparison to seeing it down below. It's unlike anything I've ever experienced before. Instead of looking at it from afar we are now a part of it. A part of the breathtaking world we always take for granted.

"It's amazing," I whisper. The cool wind whispers over every bare inch of my flesh, blowing a few strands of hair from my ponytail as we soar across the clear blue sky. "It's like we're really flying."

"That's because we are."

I finally tear my gaze away from the incredible view to look at Jase and find him watching me, a soft smile on his handsome face that has my heart tumbling in my chest.

I place a kiss on his lips, my thumb smoothing over the soft flesh after. "Thank you. Thank you for taking me here and convincing me to do this. It's the most incredible thing I've ever done."

"You're welcome."

Smiling, I turn my head forward again and enjoy the rest of our time together. Living in one of the most incredible, freeing moments of my life.

Later that evening, we're parked at a remote spot in the mountains— out in the middle of nowhere—sitting in the bed of Jase's truck with a pizza between us that we picked up after meeting Bert for his truck. Birds flock and chirp across the pink lit sky as the sun slowly sinks beyond the horizon, creating the most beautiful glow.

I didn't think anything could compare to the stunning scenery I'd already experienced today but I was wrong. The sunset paints the sky in stunning shades of gold, pink, and blue. If there was ever something prettier, it's this right here.

"How did you find this place?" I ask softly.

"My dad and I came across it a few years ago on a camping trip."

I smile, loving that he decided to share it with me. "Do you guys camp often?"

He shakes his head. "Nah. We used to but not anymore. It's hard with my schedule at the station."

"When did you decide that you wanted to be a firefighter?" I ask, wanting to know more about him, especially about his job. After my time at the station, I'm fascinated by what they do and also find it very admirable.

He glances over at me, his expression thoughtful. "You know the saying, you don't pick the job, the job picks you?"

I nod.

"Well, in my case, I think that's true. Firefighting is what I'm meant to do. I can remember as a kid, we lived down the street from the station and whenever the sirens went off I would rush over to the window and watch as the trucks headed out. Even back then my blood would rush with excitement and the need to want to be a part of it."

"That's how I feel about teaching. When I was a little girl, I would wear my grandmother's big black-rimmed glasses and make my brother and sister be my students. Sawyer always got in trouble and earned himself detention," I tell him with a laugh, but it softens into a smile as I remember the things my brother would do to appease me.

"That doesn't surprise me, he's always been an attention whore," he says, biting back a smile but we both know he means it.

"Watch it, Crawford. No one calls my brother names but me…and his wife is entitled too since she has to live with him."

"Ah yes, the famous Grace. I remember her."

"I'll bet you do since you flirted with her just to piss Sawyer off," I grumble.

"Lies, it's all lies."

I give him a dubious look, telling him I know better. My brother may be to blame for some of their bad blood but definitely not all of it. It goes both ways.

He chuckles. "All right, subject change, Peaches."

"Good idea. Let's get back to you since I'm sure it's your favorite subject."

"I wouldn't say it's my favorite. Probably my second favorite," he says, his sexy lips curling with amusement.

I have a feeling his *favorite* involves a lot of touching… Just the thought has my body flushing with desire.

I take a swig of my cold soda, hoping to cool down my raging hormones and decide to switch the subject to something safer. "How long have you been paragliding for?"

"Since the day I turned eighteen. My friends and I did it for my birthday. The first time I leaped off that mountain, I was hooked. There's nothing like it."

"You're an adrenaline junkie," I say, knowing it's true. Probably another reason he loves firefighting so much.

"Yep and it drives my mother crazy," he admits with a chuckle.

"I'll bet it does, especially when it's her only child."

"Well, her and my dad got it right the first time around so they didn't need to have more."

I quirk a brow at his bold arrogance. "So what does that say about me being the third child?"

"They stopped at you because they finally got it right."

My heart warms at the compliment, even if he is wrong. "Actually, I was…shall we say, a surprise. Although, if you ask my parents they'll tell you it was fate." A sad smile touches my lips as I think about them.

"You miss them a lot, don't you?"

I nod. "Very much. It's why I've decided to move."

"Why didn't you go with them in the first place?" There's no judgment in his tone, only genuine curiosity.

Looking away, I focus on the fuchsia sky and let out a soft breath. "I don't know. I guess I figured it was time to let go. Sawyer enlisted in the Navy when he turned eighteen and never came back except for holidays and the occasional visit. Jesse held out a bit longer, but I always knew she'd spread her wings eventually. She's far too talented to be stuck here forever. So, when my parents decided to move closer to Sawyer and his family, I knew it was my turn, but my heart wasn't ready. I mean, I know that's what life is all about, growing up, moving on, standing on your own two feet, but it has always seemed so cruel to me."

"Why do you say that?" he asks, his voice quieter than it was a moment ago.

I shrug but keep my gaze focused ahead. "I guess it hurts because while they've all found their place—their home—it's one without me. Don't get me wrong, I'm happy for them. I really am. But…they are the only ones I've ever known. And if I'm being honest, I don't want a new one. I want the one I had," I whisper, my throat beginning to burn as I reveal to him what I've never voiced to anyone before.

"Just because we get older, Sam, and our lives change, it doesn't mean we don't still belong to the family we grew up with. Hell, if it was up to my mom I'd still live at home. And to be honest, I wouldn't mind. My laundry would be done all the time and I'd be well fed but it would put a huge damper on my sex life so…"

I burst out laughing, my heavy heart feeling a bit lighter. His smile indicates that was his intention.

Staring back at him, I rest my head back on the truck. "Why did you choose this?"

"What do you mean?" he asks, confused by the sudden change of topic.

"Out of all the things we could have done today, why did you take me paragliding? Why bring me here?" I ask, gesturing to the incredible view before us.

I expect a cocky comeback but instead, he says something that I will remember for the rest of my life. "Because if anyone deserves to experience the beautiful things this world has to offer, it's you."

It's probably the kindest thing anyone has ever said to me. I give him a watery smile, my eyes burning with emotion, but I do my damnedest to blink it back. "I must admit, Crawford, for a guy who never dates you sure do know how to show a girl a good time," I tell him, hoping to lighten the moment.

He doesn't let me.

Instead, he reaches out his hand to me, his intense eyes pinning me in place. "Come here, Sam." His voice is suddenly darker—smoother. It has a commanding undertone to it that does so many amazing things to my insides.

I place my hand in his, that deep feeling of trust invading my soul as I allow him to pull me over. My knees straddle either side of his hips, and I have to bite back a moan at the feel of his impressive erection between my thighs.

His fingers dig into my hips while his gaze holds mine in the quiet dark. "I want to see you again."

Surprise flares inside of me but disappointment quickly follows. "I'm not so sure that's a good idea," I whisper, even though my heart leaps at the thought of spending more time with him.

"Why?"

"Because I'm leaving soon and it might be hard to do if I start to like you," I tell him honestly.

His lips kick up in a sexy smirk, sending a tingling sensation throughout my entire body. "Are you saying you don't like me now?"

I shrug. "Maybe a little."

He chuckles at my admission but quickly sobers. "I'd never ask you to stay. I know how much it means to you to be with your family but I want you before you go," he says, surprising me once more. His hand skims up my arm to curl around my neck and pull me in close, the warmth of his breath dancing across my lips. "No strings, no promises, and no commitments...except one."

"What's that?" I ask, my voice breathless.

"You're mine. You belong to me and only me. I don't share—ever." His voice is firmer, more possessive, sending a shiver of pleasure down my spine.

"And what about you, Jase? Will you be mine? Because I don't share either."

I'll never be second best again.

"Why the hell would I want anyone else if I have you?"

My heart swells in my chest, my cheeks hurting from smiling so big. "Good answer."

"Is that a yes?"

I nod. "Yes."

Without another word, he closes the distance between us, taking my mouth in a searing kiss that sets my body ablaze within seconds. My arms lock around his neck as I succumb to all the feelings this man evokes in me.

He cups my bottom possessively, his growl vibrating against my lips as I grind down on his erection. His hands move to the hem of my tank top and he begins sliding the material up my body. I pull back only enough to lift my arms and let him slip the shirt over my head.

His eyes darken further as they lock on the bright red push-up bra with the jeweled clasp resting between my breasts. "This is a really nice fucking bra." His voice is husky, his hands molding to the lace while he leans in to trail his lips down the column of my throat.

I grip his shoulders with a sigh, my head tilting to the side, offering him more. "I'm glad you approve. I bought it with you in mind," I tell him, desire thick in my voice. "It's fire engine red."

"It's my new favorite color… Actually, I take that back. Peach is still my favorite but this is my second."

My giggle is cut off when he curves an arm around my waist and takes me to my back, coming over top of me. The hard ridge of his jeans nudging me where I want him most. I arch up with a moan, thankful for the soft blanket beneath me.

Gripping the fabric of his shirt, I begin dragging it up his sculpted back. Once it clears his head, a subtle gasp leaves me at the feel of his warm, bare skin against mine. The connection steals my breath, sending an army of sensations to implode across my body.

"Tonight, I'm taking my time with you. I'm going to learn every inch of your body and fucking own it."

One piece at a time, he removes the remainder of my clothes. With every inch of skin exposed, his eyes grow heavier, filling with the intense need that always pulls me in. His warm lips not only taste and explore but they worship and cherish every piece of me before latching onto my aching center.

I cry out, my fingers curling in his hair, hips bucking up against his skilled mouth as the most exquisite pleasure explodes through me.

"Goddamn, you have the sweetest pussy I've ever tasted, baby." The dirty words only add to the sensations taking over my body.

My heated moans and cries of pleasure fill the night air as he devours me. It isn't long before he finds that perfect spot, the one that pushes me into divine oblivion. His name pours from my lips, bouncing with a soft echo off the mountains surrounding us.

As I float down from the high, he crawls back up, dropping a kiss on my tummy, my hip, between my breasts, before capturing my mouth in a fiery kiss and sliding into me in one smooth motion.

The connection slams into me with the same ferocity as last time.

My gasp and his groan mingle in the same breath as he completes a part of me I never knew I had. One that feels like it's been reserved only for him, but how can that be? How can someone I barely know make me feel this way? It's more than two bodies coming together; it's the joining of two souls.

Unlike last time, there's nothing rushed about it. Instead, he moves inside of me with slow precision, each stroke deeper than the last, his muscles straining beneath my fingertips. I open my eyes, the sky littered with a million stars sparkling above us and again that niggling feeling pulls at me. One so strong I could swear I've done this before, with him. It feels right. And for the the first time in a long time, I finally feel like I'm exactly where I'm meant to be.

I pray, when it comes time to say good-bye, I will be able to walk away with my heart still intact. Because as of right now, he is stealing it from me. One moment at a time.

CHAPTER 10

Jase

Sitting around the kitchen table, we chow down on a steak dinner that the captain was forced to buy since he lost in poker last week. Don Gyepesi, or whom we call Captain Gypsy, can be a cynical, grumpy bastard. He's put in many years and is close to his retirement but I don't see him going anywhere any time soon. Other than my father, I respect no man more than him. He's dedicated his life to this profession and he's trained some of the best. He's taught us all we know.

Tonight, we also have Mikey sharing our meal with us. He's a special needs boy who has been coming to this station as long as I have worked here. He helps out where he can and we accept him as one of our own. Whenever we get a call he closes up behind us and waits by the radio until we get back.

"How's your steak, Mikey?" Austin asks.

Since his mouth is full, his response is a thumbs-up.

"Mikey likes it," Cam mocks, sending a collection of chuckles around the table.

Feeling my cell phone vibrate in my pocket, I reach in and pull it out to see a text from Sam. When I open the message, a picture of a basket of peaches pops up that says, *got peaches?*

Chuckling, I'm just about to reply when another message from her comes up.

Sam: *Serious question, Crawford. Do you really like peaches?*

I bite back a groan as I think about how much.

Me: *Yeah, baby, as long as they come from you, I like them. Why?*

Sam: *Because I'm going to make something when you come over for supper on Friday, but I won't bother if you really don't like them.*

Me: *Just spread your legs when I get there and I'll fucking love them.*

Thinking about the taste of her pussy has my cock hardening. I've come to learn everything about this girl is sweet. Her scent, her laugh, the sexy fucking noises she makes when I'm eating her out…

The ding of another text snaps me out of my perverted thoughts.

Sam: *I'm rolling my eyes right now…and maybe blushing at the image that just popped in my head.*

Me fucking, too. The heat rushing through my veins right now is not something I care to be experiencing while I'm sitting at a table with a bunch of dudes.

Me: *Can we pick this up later? The guys and I are eating supper right now, and I really don't want to explain why I'm sporting a hard-on.*

Sam: *LOL! Yes, tell the boys I said hi and if there is any peach dessert left on Friday I'll send some their way.*

Me: *We've talked about this. No one gets your peaches but me.*

Sam: **eye roll* Bye, Crawford, see you soon.*

Not soon enough.

I crave this girl every second of every day. For the past two weeks I've been with her every chance I get. When I'm not here, I'm buried in her, losing myself not only in her body but everything else about her. I don't know how the hell I'm going to be able to say good-bye when the time comes.

I quickly shove the thought aside, not wanting to think about it. Slipping my phone back into my pocket, I look up to see everyone at the table staring at me. "What?"

"You have it so fucking bad," Cam says, shaking his head with a chuckle.

A collection of agreements follow from everyone else around the table.

"You don't know what the hell you're talking about," I grumble.

"No? Are you telling me the stupid grin that was just on your face has nothing to do with a certain blonde haired, green eyed bombshell that, might I add, just so happens to be Sawyer Evans's baby sister?"

I tense, cutting a glare his way. "Watch it, Phillips. That asshole has nothing to do with Sam and me."

"Then what does it have to do with, Crawford?" Jake asks, his accusing tone instantly pissing me off.

"What's it to you, *Ryan*?"

"Sam is cool regardless of how you feel about her brother. If this is some sort of fucking vendetta against him then—"

"I just said he has nothing to do with it. This is between Sam and me. So mind your own fucking business."

"All right, both of you, calm the fuck down," Austin snaps, his voice coming through louder than the two of ours. "Look, Crawford, we're just surprised is all. It's no secret you don't like that family, Sam included."

"When the hell did I ever say I didn't like her?"

"Whenever you'd run into her you'd do everything you could to piss her off. That was indication enough," he says.

"That's because he wanted to fuck her," Cam cuts back in, earning himself another glare from me. "What? It's not like it isn't true. Anytime both of you were in the same room you could cut the tension with a knife. The same tension Austin and our girl Zoey has," he adds. "Except theirs isn't so…shall we say…volatile."

Austin sits back in his chair, his eyes narrowing at Cam's smug smirk. "Since when the hell did you become a fucking expert on love?"

"Hey, who said anything about love? I'm talking about attraction and fucking, and for your information, I know a lot about that shit."

We all grunt but don't argue. It's no secret he's the biggest whore of us all.

Before anyone can say more, Captain Gypsy comes storming in. "What the hell is all the griping about? I'm on a goddamn phone call and I hear you all fighting like a bunch of girls. Shut up and eat the damn dinner I paid for."

Silence fills the air as he stomps away, the sound of his boots hitting the hard floor before we hear the slam of his door.

We all share a look before busting out in laughter.

"Shut up and eat the damn dinner I paid for," Declan mocks, making us laugh harder.

Once we wind down, I decide to lay the prior issue to rest once and for all. "Look, I get you guys care about Sam but you know me better than that. I'd never use her to get to him. It's not my style."

Although, I hate to admit it but I did entertain the idea once years ago. It was shortly after he fucked Stephanie, but I came to my senses quick. And thank God for that. Because the thought of hurting her or causing her pain makes me sick to my stomach, especially now that I've gotten to know her.

"You're right," Jake says. "I do know you better. Just be prepared, because you know if Evans gets wind of this he's going to think the same thing."

I don't care what that asshole thinks. He can mind his own fucking business, too.

"Can I say something?" Cam asks.

"No!" we all answer at once.

"Well, I'm going to fucking say it anyway," he starts, talking over our groans. "I think it's time you and Evans put this shit to rest. Now that Sam is involved someone is bound to get hurt, and I have a feeling it won't be either of you."

There will never be a truce between Evans and me. There's too much history. Too much bad blood between us. We can't erase what's been done between us, but none of that has anything to do with Sam.

"I think that might have been one of the most intellectual things you've ever said, Phillips," Austin says, breaking into my thoughts.

"Told you assholes I know what I'm talking about."

Another round of chuckles fill the room but I remain silent, that deep-seated hate bubbling to the surface but I shove it back down.

For the next few weeks she's mine and no one, including her brother, is going to stop me from soaking up every single minute I can with her.

CHAPTER 11

Sam

My thoughts are consumed with Jase as I sit on my lunch break in-between classes on Friday afternoon. Our time together hasn't been long but it's been more than I could hope for. If we're not making love then he's making me laugh or holding me in his strong arms until dawn breaks and it's time for him to leave. Every moment spent with him is better than the last and it feels so...easy...natural even. It's like we've known each other for years.

I guess we have but not like this. Not by touch or kiss. That's all new but for some reason my heart remembers it—remembers something it never had. How is it possible to know someone's touch before you ever felt it? I can't explain it, and I don't think I will ever be able to.

I know I need to keep my heart out of this but it's getting harder. I can't fall in love with him. I absolutely can't. I'm moving and it's something I'm not going to change my mind about. Besides, our families hate each other. I can't imagine what a family dinner would be like.

I don't even want to think about it.

Sighing, I grab my cell phone out of my purse and put in a call to Grace's bakery.

She answers on the third ring. "A Slice of Hope with a Sprinkle of Grace, this is Grace speaking, how can I help you?"

"Grace, it's Sam."

"Sam, what a pleasant surprise," she says, genuine happiness in her tone. "How are you?"

"I'm good, how about you guys? How are my niece and nephew?"

"They are wonderful and very excited for you to finally get here. We all are."

"Me, too," I say, though it lacks my usual enthusiasm.

"So what do I owe this pleasure?"

"Do you have a minute?"

"Of course."

"I need a peach pie recipe. The best one you have."

"Oh, brushing up on your skills so you can help your sister-in-law out when ya get here?" she asks hopefully.

"I'll come and help out anytime but we both know it won't taste nearly as good as yours or even Hope's for that matter." My precious little niece is almost as good as her mom.

"Nonsense. You will be great. I can't wait to see you. I've missed you so dang much. We all have."

"I miss you all, too," I tell her, my heart swelling in my chest.

"Okay, I'm going to give you a pretty simple recipe but I want you to have fun with it. Add things. Toss some of your favorites in it then name it whatever you want. Don't hold back, even if it ends up tasting terrible. You'll know what to do differently for next time."

I smile at the excitement in her voice, her passion igniting one of my own. It's contagious. "Okay, I will."

I jot down the list of ingredients and simple directions. After she finishes she asks what the special occasion is.

"Actually, it's for a date," I say carefully.

She gasps. "Really? Oh my gosh, that's so darn excitin'. Anyone I know?"

I shift in my seat, unsure of whether to tell her or not. I hate to put her in a bad place since she would have to keep it from Sawyer.

"Are you sure you want to know the answer to that?" I ask.

"Well, I most certainly do now." She laughs.

"Promise not to tell my brother?"

There's a long bout of silence.

"Uh-oh. That doesn't sound good. Maybe not."

"It's probably better you don't," I say softly.

"It's not Grant, is it?"

"No. Not at all."

"Oh good. Well...oh the heck with it. Tell me anyway or I'll die from curiosity."

"It's Jase Crawford."

"Holy Toledo," she shrieks. "Are you messin' with me right now?"

A soft sigh escapes me. "No. And I know what you're thinking."

"Oh, I'm not so sure you do."

"You think it's a mistake, just like Jesse. But if it is, Grace, it's the best one I've ever made. It's nothing serious," I add, not only lying to her but myself. What I feel for Jase is serious, more than I care to admit. But I'm sticking to the deal, even if it kills me. "We're just spending time with each other before I move, and...it's been really great. I haven't been this happy in a long time."

"Oh, Sam. I can hear it in your voice," she says softly, her words parallel to Jesse's. "If he's good to you and you're happy then that's all that matters."

"He is...real good to me."

"I believe it. I only met him that one time, and it's one I will never bring up around your brother or it'll set him off."

I cringe just thinking of my brother's reaction.

"Lord knows none of us needs to see that," she continues. "But even in the short time that I met him, I could tell Jase was a good guy. He actually reminded me a lot of Sawyer, which is why I think they butt heads so much. The world isn't big enough for both of their egos."

I chuckle. "Now that I agree with."

There's a thoughtful pause between the both of us.

"You know, something my mama always said was to let your heart lead you and you can never go wrong. Follow it, Sam, and see where you end up."

My throat thickens at the sound of her sad voice as she talks about her late mother. "Thanks, Grace."

"Anytime. Let me know how your pie turns out."

"I will. I'll call you back this weekend."

"Sounds good. Take care."

"You, too."

The rest of my day passes in a blur, Jase never far from my thoughts or heart.

Once the last child is picked up, I rush out of the school and drive straight to the u-pick farm that's located just on the outskirts of town, wanting to get the freshest peaches for my pie. It's owned by the McNallys, a sweet elderly couple who have been longtime residents of Silver Creek.

Unfortunately, when I pull up, Mr. and Mrs. McNally are parked outside the metal gate, locking up the property.

Shoot! They're closed already?

Mrs. McNally waves to me while sitting in her car as she waits for Mr. McNally to finish locking up.

Waving back, I put the car in park and step out, keeping one foot inside.

"Well hello, Miss Samantha," Mr. McNally greets me.

I try not to cringe at the use of my full name. I never liked it much before, but since Grant I do even less now.

"Hi, Mr. and Mrs. McNally," I greet them both with a smile. "I guess this means you guys are closed for the day?"

He gives me a regretful nod. "I know it's a little early but we have our granddaughter's year end recital this evening."

"How lovely," I tell him. "Well, no problem. I was hoping to pick some fresh peaches but the grocery store will just have to do. Have a nice time."

I'm about to climb back into my car when Mrs. McNally calls out to me. "Samantha, dear, you're welcome to go on in if you don't mind locking up after yourself."

"Really? Are you sure that would be okay?"

"Absolutely."

"Thank you. I won't be long. I promise."

Shutting off my car, I grab my wicker basket that sits on the passenger seat then hurry over to hand Mr. McNally twenty dollars, but he waves me away.

"Don't worry about it. This time is on us."

"Oh no. I insist. Especially when you are gracious enough to trust me alone here."

"Of course we do, dear. You were raised by some of the best people I know."

I smile, my heart warming at the compliment. No matter how hard I push for him to accept the money, he refuses.

"You go on now," Mrs. McNally says. "The trees are in the far back corner. There should be a small ladder close by. You'll find the ripest ones at the top."

I nod. "Thank you again."

After bidding me farewell, they drive away, their station wagon disappearing down the dusty road. Leaving my car parked where it is, I walk up the long gravel driveway, admiring the beautiful scenery as I make my way to the back of the property. The grass is green and lush, the trees and shrubs full of bright, rich, colorful fruits.

When I finally make it to the peach trees, I seek out the fullest one and choose the middle. Slipping my phone in the pocket of my vintage, knee-length, gingham skirt, I begin pulling peaches from the branches that I can reach, having to stretch up on my tiptoes, but quickly notice how firm they are.

Craning my head back, I see that Mrs. McNally is right; the plumpest ones seem to be at the top. I grab the wooden ladder that lies against one of the other trees and bring it over. After placing my wicker basket on the ground, I start my climb. Halfway up my ankle almost rolls, thanks to the heels I'm wearing.

Probably not the smartest thing to wear when climbing a ladder.

Once I make it to the top step, I carefully reach up and pick a few more; happy they are softer than the other ones I picked below. I step down close enough to gently place them in the basket then make the climb again and stretch up to grab another. That's when I spot a large plump one that sits all by itself, much higher up, just begging to be picked.

Against my better judgment, I step up onto the platform, the ladder beginning to shake from my wobbly legs.

Crap, not a good idea.

Just when I'm about to climb back down, the ladder tilts beneath me. With a shriek of panic, I reach out for the thick, heavy branch and grab hold of it while the ladder clatters to the ground.

"Oh shit. This is not good." Fear thrums through my veins when I look down, to see just how far up I am. "This is really not good."

Stay calm, Sam. Think.

With all the strength I possess, I swing my lower body up and lock my legs around the thick branch, uncaring how indecent I look with my skirt flipped up, showcasing my ass to all of Mother Nature.

Eventually, I manage to twist up enough to situate myself on top, straddling the rough bark before I plummet to my death. I glance down once more and groan at the tipped over ladder.

"Great. How the hell am I going to get down?"

Taking in my surroundings, I see if I can climb my way back down but none of the branches seem as sturdy as the one I'm on. With my luck today, I'm liable to break my neck. Not having any other choice, I reach for my cell phone, thankful it didn't fall out in the midst of my epic tree swinging skills, and call Zoey. But she doesn't answer.

"No, no, no. Please, don't be unavailable now. Please."

I call three more times, only to get her voicemail. I try my other friend, Monica, who I deem more of an acquaintance but she doesn't answer either. It makes me want to cry because it means I'm stuck having to call the last person I want to come here and find me like this.

Someone who will never let me live it down.

Shoving aside my pride, I punch in his number. Of course he answers on the first ring.

"Peaches," he greets me in that deep, sexy voice of his. "I'm just packing up to leave, I'll be over soon."

"Would you mind making a stop first?"

"Sure. What do you need?"

"Help," I tell him cryptically.

"Huh?"

I release a humiliated breath. "I need help. I'm stuck."

"What?" he snaps, concern thick in his voice. "What do you mean you're stuck? In your car? Are you hurt? Were you in an accident?"

"No. It's nothing like that. I'm not hurt. Well…maybe my pride," I grumble. "Look, can you just come out to the McNally farm. I'm at the back left end of the property. I'll explain when you get here."

"Hang tight. I'm on my way."

Oh I'll be hanging all right.

Ending the call, I rest against the rough bark and look up to see the reason why I'm in this mess in the first place. Reaching up, I pluck the lone peach and glare at it. "This is all your fault," I grumble before taking a miserable bite.

By the yumminess that explodes in my mouth, it's almost worth it—almost.

CHAPTER 12

Jase

I pull up to the McNally farm and see Sam's car parked out front but without her in it. Worry burns in my gut as I jog to the back of the property where she said she would be, but I still don't see her. However, I do find a tipped over ladder, a basket full of peaches, and a pair of pink heels.

What the hell?

When a peach falls out of the sky and hits me in the shoulder, I glance up to find the girl I'm looking for. Sam gazes down at me with a small, embarrassed smile, her hair a tangled mess around her pretty face and those sparkling eyes of hers more pronounced in the lush green tree.

A tree filled with peaches.

If I didn't know better I'd swear I was dreaming, but in my dreams she would be naked in that tree.

"Hi," she greets me softly.

"What the fuck are you doing up there?" I ask, trying to hold back my amusement when it's clear she's distressed.

A tortured groan escapes her. "You're never going to believe this."

She begins telling me the whole story, starting from when she showed up and the McNallys let her in alone, her mouth moving a million miles a minute.

"So here I am, picking the best peaches I can find when I see this one all the way up here on its own. Well, now I know why. Because in order to get it you have to do risky things. Things that could kill you. I, of course, took the risk. It wasn't very Sensible Sam of me, and I paid the price. The ladder fell out beneath me but I caught this big branch, just barely escaping my imminent death," she explains, holding up her thumb and finger an inch apart. "If you breathe a word of this to anyone, Crawford, I will make you die a slow and painful death."

By the time she finishes her fucking babbling, I'm laughing my ass off.

It doesn't take long for her to join in but hers sounds not only embarrassed but also has a little crazy mixed in there, too. "Oh my god, Jase, I know it's ridiculous. Just please get me down from here. I've almost been stung by a bee three times. The little bastard won't leave me alone."

"Because bees like sweet things and there's nothing sweeter than you, baby."

She glares down at me. "Now is not the time to be charming, Crawford. Get me down."

"All right, hold on." I set up the ladder and climb halfway up, still chuckling at this ridiculous situation.

She turns around to step down, searching for the platform with her foot. Grabbing her smooth bare ankle, I help her find it and stay close to ensure she doesn't slip. Once I know she's good, I step back down but stand at the bottom to hold the ladder steady, trying my damnedest to get a peek at what she has on beneath this classy fucking skirt of hers.

Thong? Or lace?

It always seems to be one or the other. I really have no preference but I can say her ass looks best without anything covering it. My curiosity gets the best of me and I lift the material to see a soft pink silk thong. A low growl rumbles from my chest, my cock hardening at the sexy sight.

"Hey! Stop that." She swats my hand away and it causes her to lose her footing. I catch her as she falls back, her high-pitched shriek filling the air.

"Jase, you asshole." She struggles in my arms, throwing tiny punches my way.

Laughing, I block her pathetic attempts and take us to the grassy ground, covering her body before claiming her mouth. I groan at the sweet taste of her, one I've missed these past few days. It's an addiction I've come to crave—need.

Her struggle comes to a stop and she instantly melts against me, her arms locking around my neck while she gives as good as she gets.

"I fucking missed you," I growl against her lips.

"Me too, so much."

Tearing my mouth away, I drag my lips down the slender column of her throat, my hand slipping under her skirt to glide up her smooth, bare thigh.

"You better stop before we get ourselves into trouble," she says breathlessly but tilts her head to the side, giving me more of what I want.

"I love trouble. Especially when it involves you and your pussy." I roll my hips, letting her feel how hard I am for her.

A fiery whimper pushes past her lips. "Stop the dirty talk, Crawford. You know what it does to me."

I chuckle, yeah, I do. She loves it dirty and it only fuels the beast inside of me. The one that wants to corrupt every part of her—ruin her for anyone else that will come after me… The thought has acid settling in my gut. To think of anyone else touching her makes me fucking violent.

Temporary, Crawford. That's the deal.

"Come on, baby. There's no one around for miles and we're surrounded by peaches. It's fate. We have to fuck here."

She laughs, the breathy sound doing shit to my chest. "As appealing as that sounds, Sensible Sam doesn't think it's a good idea."

"Forget Sensible Sam. Lock her up and bring out my favorite Sam."

"And which one is that?" I can hear the smile in her voice while I continue to nip and suck at her sensitive flesh.

"The one who screams my name while she's coming on my cock.

She's my favorite."

Her laughter trails off into a heated moan, her hips lifting, driving me to the brink of insanity.

I pull back to look down at her. "Is that a yes?"

She scans our surroundings, her teeth sinking into her bottom lip. "What if they have cameras out here?"

"There's no cameras out here, baby. We would see them if there were."

She thinks about it for only a second then tugs me down closer and grants me the permission I've been dying to hear. "Make it quick, Crawford. And we better not end up on the Internet for this."

Growling, I flip her to her stomach and lift her to her knees. "Don't worry, baby, I'll make this fast but so fucking good."

"I have no doubt it will be good," she says, her breaths quick and fast. "It always is."

Damn straight it is. Because it's us. I've always loved to fuck but nothing has ever felt as good as it does to be inside of this girl. It's in a league all on its own.

Lifting her skirt, my hand smooths over one bare, round globe. "You have no idea the shit I want to do to this body of yours."

"I think I have an idea or two."

"No, I don't think you do, but you will soon because I plan to invade every inch of this body so you'll never be able to forget me."

She starts to say something but trails off on a gasp when I lay a soft hand against her flesh, the slight smack echoing in the air around us.

A harsh moan falls from her as she pushes back for more.

I give her another tap, this one a little harder, watching her pale flesh stain pink.

"Oh god," she whimpers, the heated sound traveling across my skin with thick desire.

I shove aside the thin silk covering her pussy, my fingers delving into her hot flesh, finding her soaked and ready for me. "You're so pretty, Sam, especially when you're greedy for my cock."

"Jase, please," she pleads, feeding the fire that's in my soul.

Unfastening my jeans, I lower them just enough to free myself then thrust home, losing myself in the most mind-numbing pleasure I've ever felt.

There is no greater feeling in the world than being inside this girl.

"You good, baby?" I ask through clenched teeth, giving her time to adjust.

"So good. Don't stop."

My fucking pleasure.

Gripping her hips, I begin fucking her hard and fast, my hips slapping against the soft flesh of her ass. Her screams of pleasure fuel me, making me feel like a fucking animal with every savage thrust.

I watch my cock disappear in and out of her gripping heat, the image sending fire racing through my blood. "Jesus, Sam, we look good right now, baby. My cock feeding this hungry little pussy of yours. It's fucking perfect."

"Jase!" she whimpers, the dirty words have her pussy gripping me tighter.

Reaching between her legs, I massage the swollen bud, giving her the push she needs. My name purges from her lips on a wail of pleasure.

"That a girl, scream for me."

I continue fucking her through her orgasm, not letting myself go until I feel the last of her tremors subside. Then I detonate—crashing over the edge hard and fast—the fiery pleasure searing my veins.

I pull out of her with a groan, wishing I could stay there forever. A smirk curls my lips when she drops to the ground with a blissful sigh. Leaning over, I press a kiss to her slender shoulder. "You okay, baby?"

"Mmm. More than okay," she mumbles before turning around to face me. With a satisfied smile, she tugs me down to what I expect will be a kiss but instead is a hug.

That's it. Just a hug—her arms holding me tight.

"About what you said earlier," she whispers. "I want you to know, I'll never forget you. Not a second of our time together. I will remember it forever."

Fire burns in my chest, working its way up my throat as I think about the day to come that I will lose her and all she will be is the sweetest memory I'll ever have.

CHAPTER 13

Sam

An hour later we're back at my apartment. Music plays on the radio as we make the pie together. Or rather, I'm making it and Jase is sampling.

"How about cinnamon? Do you think that would taste good?" I ask him, trying to think of some other ingredients to make it my own. I've already added a dash of nutmeg, ginger, and brown sugar. I'm going with a fall spice type theme. If it turns out good I could make it for Thanksgiving this year.

"Toss it in and I'll tell you," he says, nuzzling the back of my neck as he stands behind me, his strong arms wrapped around my waist.

With a smile, I sprinkle some into the mix. His hand encircles my wrist then lifts it to dip my finger into the yummy gooeyness before sucking it off. It has goose bumps crawling up my arm. I just had the most mind-blowing sex only a short time ago and already my body is on fire for him again.

"Yep, it's fucking delicious," he groans.

"It's a good thing no one else is eating this pie but us." I giggle. "It's definitely not up to standards in the sanitary department."

"Damn straight! Nobody gets your pie but me."

I shake my head but can't deny the way my insides melt at his possessiveness. After pouring the filling into the piecrust that I already made, I take the strips of dough I have sitting off to the side and crisscross them over top. Then I put the finishing touch by adding the heart in the center that I had cut out earlier with a small cookie cutter.

"There. Now even if it ends up tasting bad it will at least look pretty," I say with a proud smile. Opening the oven, I slide it inside then set the timer. "Now we just need to come up with a name." I turn around to find Jase watching me with that sexy smirk of his, hunger prominent in his dark eyes.

Stepping closer, he hooks an arm around my waist and yanks me against his hard body before laying one heck of a kiss on me.

"Hmmm, maybe Peach Kiss Pie?" I suggest with a breathy sigh.

"Or Jase is Sexy Pie. I like that one."

A laugh tumbles past my lips, my arms encircling his neck. "You are so arrogant, Jase Crawford. Yet…also truthful."

Lifting me off my feet, he sits me on the counter and comes to stand between my open legs. "And you are beautiful, Samantha Evans."

I tense, the starting of his words that warmed my soul ending with what feels like a bucket of ice-cold water. "Sam," I whisper. "Always just Sam. Okay?"

"Why not Samantha? It's a pretty name, especially when it comes with a face like yours."

His sweet words ease the heaviness of my heart. "I've always preferred Sam, or Sammy…but only if you're my dad," I tell him with a smile but it fades quickly with what I say next. "Grant always used it to scold me like a child. Now it gives me the chills when I hear it."

His eyes darken with rage, the same one I saw explode from him the night he unleashed it on Grant. "Tell me to mind my own business if you want, but I've been wondering how the hell you ended up with a piece of shit like him."

Humiliation burns inside of me. "Pathetic, huh?"

"No. Not pathetic. I just know the fire you have in you. You don't put up with any shit. So why did you put up with his?"

"You wouldn't understand."

How could he when I don't even understand it myself?

"Try me."

Letting out a heavy sigh, I try my best to explain. "When I look back on it now I feel so stupid. Naïve even, but he was good. He found my weaknesses and nipped at them constantly, stripping away my confidence one insult at a time, but he was smart about it. Subtle at first. Eventually, it got worse, and to the point where I suddenly felt trapped. He made me feel like I had no one, when in reality I had everyone. He used my family against me often."

"How so?" he asks, his voice tight.

"My entire life, I've always lived in Sawyer's and Jesse's shadows. Which isn't a bad thing," I rush to say. "Honestly, I preferred it. But at times, I felt like I lacked compared to them and Grant knew that. He used it against me every chance he got." Pain strikes my heart as I remember all the cruel and hurtful things he would say to me.

"How the hell could you think you lacked in any way?"

I shrug. "My brother and sister always stood out. Sawyer's funny and charismatic. He can walk into a room and make everyone instantly fall in love with him—"

His grunt cuts me off.

"Well, almost anyone." I chuckle, remembering whom I'm talking to. "Then there's Jesse who was born as talented as they come. Her eye for fashion and skill of what she can do with a piece of material is nothing short of a masterpiece. Even from the time she was a little girl, her talent shined so bright." There's no hostility only affection as I talk about my sister. "Then, there was me. Wearing my grandma's glasses, playing teacher," I say, but it's with a smile. "Don't get me wrong. I like who I am but I have never shone like them. I've always just been…Sensible Sam."

"You shine so fucking bright it's blinding," he says, making my heart skip a beat. His large hand slips under my hair to cup my cheek. "I also happen to really like Sensible Sam. She's beautiful," he whispers, leaning in to kiss my temple. "Sweet," he adds, moving to the corner of my eye. "And she's my favorite in the Evans family."

"That's because you don't like anyone in my family." I chuckle but it's halfhearted.

"That's not true. I don't know your parents, and I may have encountered Jesse over the years but make no mistake, Sam. Not once did she ever stop my fucking heart from beating when she walked by like you do. No one ever has."

I gaze back at him, his admission catching me by surprise. "Has it always been like that?" I ask bravely, terrified for his answer.

"Yeah. Always. Even when I didn't want it to be."

His words are like a soothing balm to my wounded heart. "For the record, Crawford. Even though I thought you were an asshole and wanted to punch you for pushing my buttons, I still thought you were hot."

An amused grin transforms his face. "I love pushing your buttons, baby. You're sexy when you get mad. Then again, I always think you're sexy. Even when you're stuck in a tree."

I drop my head on his shoulder, my laughter trailing into a groan. "Don't remind me."

"Don't worry. Your secret is safe with me."

"I have a feeling I'm always safe with you," I whisper, my heart full of contentment.

"Yeah, you are." His strong arms hug me closer, bringing me a peace I've grown to depend on. "What made you finally leave him?" he asks quietly, coming back to the subject that started it all.

"I showed up at his office one night when he was *working late* and found him fucking his secretary."

I feel him tense, his muscles coiling tight around me. "Jesus, what a fucking loser."

"I wasn't that surprised. I had a feeling all along. The way women would look at me whenever I had to accompany him to a business function always made my stomach churn. He would lie and play it off like they had a thing for him but I always knew better. It was just another one of his ways of making me feel like I was lucky to have him."

I shake my head, my blood heating at the memory.

"I was angry and humiliated. But most of all, I was relieved. It was finally my way out."

"You always had a way out, Sam."

"I know that now but at the time I was scared—really scared. He has a bad temper, as you know, and it terrified me."

"He's a fucking coward. Anyone who picks on someone smaller than them is."

I nod. "You're right, and eventually I learned that. He's a mistake I will regret for the rest of my life. But I also learned a lot about myself in those dark months, and I became stronger for it. It helped me realize what I really want in life."

"And what's that?"

"Someone that will love me for who I am," I tell him quietly, remembering how Grant tried to change everything about me.

"Only a fool wouldn't fall in love with you, Sam."

I still, a small flare of hope igniting inside of me. "It's more than just loving me. I need someone who will respect my feelings when it comes to my family," I tell him, treading into dangerous territory when it comes to us. "We've been through a lot together, more than anyone could possibly understand. Especially when it comes to Sawyer."

His brows draw in confusion. "How do you mean?"

I swallow thickly as I think about that call so many years ago. The one I thought would destroy us all. "You know how Sawyer joined the Navy?"

He nods.

"Five years into his service we got a call that's every family's worst nightmare. He and two of his friends, Cade being one of them," I tell him since he knows who he is, "were held captive and tortured. So badly that they were unrecognizable."

"Jesus," he breathes, surprise heavy in his voice.

Tears blur my vision as I remember that day so vividly. "I'll never forget that call for as long as I live. The sound of my mother's grief-stricken scream when she answered. The way she fell to her knees in agony, I thought for sure he was dead. I was so relieved when I found out he wasn't…until I went and saw him in the hospital in Germany," I whisper, my throat on fire now. "I know how horrible this sounds but at the time, seeing how badly he was hurt, I almost thought it would have been better for him if he had. He suffered so badly. It took nine months of rehabilitation before he healed, but some things you never recover from. And the scars he bears to this day, I'm sure, are far less than the ones he will forever have inside of him."

"I'm sorry, Sam," he says, brushing his knuckles across my wet cheek. "Even though we don't get along, I hope you know I wouldn't wish that on him."

I meet his gaze, my tears falling faster. "I do know that, but I wish you knew him for the man he really is. He's not perfect but he really is a good person."

He drops his forehead on mine, his jaw flexing, but I'm not sure if it's in anger or frustration. "Some people just don't mesh, baby, and that's us." My heart breaks a little more even though he's just being honest with me. "But there is one thing I've always liked about him."

"What's that?" I ask on a whisper.

"You."

I smile, that one word easing the heaviness in my chest. He turns to look at the timer on the oven, seeing there's still forty minutes left.

"Are you hungry?" I ask, thinking we should order in since my supper preparation was ruined by my adventure at the orchard.

His dark eyes swing back to mine, the heat in his gaze warming me from the inside out. "Yeah, but not for food." He lifts me off the counter, catching me by surprise.

My arms wrap around his neck and legs around his waist as he carries me into my room. "I like where your head's at, Crawford."

"Just wait until you see what I'm about to do with my dick, you're going to love it."

I burst out laughing as he tosses me on my bed and comes over top of me, the weight of him a familiar comfort I've grown accustomed to.

He stares down at me, his expression soft with amusement yet something else, something I can't quite put my finger on.

"What?" I ask, my smile softening.

"I could listen to you laugh everyday for the rest of my life."

My heart misses a beat, those beautiful words creating a storm of emotions inside of me. I would love nothing more than to share every laugh, tear, and smile with him for the rest of my life, but I fear he hates my brother too much to love me.

Before I'm able to voice that he captures my mouth in a searing kiss that burns me all the way down to my soul, obliterating everything and everyone in this world but us.

For now it's enough. It has to be.

CHAPTER 14

Sam

Tears stream down my face as I sit at my desk, reading all the homemade cards and sweet gifts my students gave me for the end of the year. I managed to maintain my composure until the last child left then erupted like a volcano.

Every year it's like this for me, but this one is even more emotional because I know I won't ever see their cute little faces again. Not even by chance at the grocery store like I do now…because I won't be here. That reality makes this so much harder.

Sniffling, I open the next card, from Jacob Wilson. *Miss Evans. Thank you for being my teacher. I love you. You're the best teacher I've ever had.*

"Oh!" A fresh wave of tears starts all over again, his messy printing and beautiful words melting my heart. Even if I am the only teacher he's ever had, it's still so damn sweet.

A knock on my open classroom door startles me out of my emotional turmoil. Looking up, I find Jase leaning against the doorframe. He holds a big bouquet of tiger lilies and wears a sympathetic smile on his handsome face.

"Hey," I greet him in surprise, wiping my wet cheeks with the back of my hand. "What are you doing here?"

He strides in, that sexy swagger of his making my heavy heart tumble in my chest. "Zoey told me today would be hard for you so I waited outside until the bell rang and all the kids left. I didn't want you to be alone."

My chest swells with love, his sweet gesture making me want to blubber all over again.

He places the flowers down on my lap then hunkers down before me, taking one of my hands in his and bringing it to his mouth for a kiss. "You okay?"

"I am now," I whisper. "Thank you for thinking of me."

"I'm always thinking about you."

His kind words wash over me, sending peace to invade my soul.

"Is it because you're going to miss them?" he asks.

"Among other people," I say softly, my hand moving to the side of his face.

His eyes darken with pain, the same one I feel all the way to my core when I think about leaving him. We haven't spoken about it. We avoid the subject because it hurts too much. But as the date quickly approaches, my heart grows heavier and the tension between us magnifies.

He turns his face in, kissing the inside of my palm. "Let's get out of here."

"Where?"

He shrugs. "The street festival downtown is happening tonight. Why don't we head there and grab dinner. It will help take your mind off things."

I smile. "Yeah, that sounds nice."

"Come here." He tugs me to stand then enfolds me in his strong arms, holding me close. We stand locked together for a long time, my face buried in his chest, silence filling the air. But we didn't need words in this moment—our hug said it all.

We aren't ready to lose this. I'm not sure if I ever will be.

Jase

We walk hand in hand, my large one engulfing her delicate one while she holds a spool of pink cotton candy in her other. Rows of booths and performers are lined up along main street. We stop to join a large group of people as they watch a guy perform with fire. He dances around, his sticks aflame, one that he ends up swallowing before breathing fire back onto it.

"Whoa!" Sam quickly becomes entranced with the show, her eyes as big as saucers. I, on the other hand, don't find him all that entertaining but that's probably because my mind is elsewhere. In a place I don't want to be, a reality I don't want to face.

In just a few short weeks she's going to be gone and there's not a damn thing I can do about it. The thought of never seeing her again has dread snaking around my chest. It coils so fucking tight that I can't take in a full breath.

I don't want her to leave. I'm not ready to lose her yet. But I won't hold her back either, not when I know how much she needs her family. I love her enough to let her go...

Whoa! Care. I *care* about her enough. Not love. I can't. It's too soon for that...right?

This wasn't supposed to happen. I was supposed to enjoy these last few months with her. Get her out of my system and move on. The problem is—there is no working her out of my system. She has left an ever-lasting mark on me that will never be erased.

I'm seriously fucked.

I'm pulled out of my thoughts when we start walking again. Sam decides to be a pain in the ass by reaching up to shove the cotton candy in my mouth but ends up getting it all over my damn face.

She lets out a squeal of laughter when I turn the tables on her, my arm hooking around her neck as I dip her back to rub the pink fluff all over hers.

"Okay, okay, stop. I'm sorry," she begs for mercy.

I remove the smudged cotton candy and cover her mouth with mine; licking up all the sticky sweetness, but the cherry-flavored candy has nothing on her.

She moans into my mouth, her arms winding around my neck. My blood ignites with heated force as I get lost in her as if we're the only two people on this crowded street.

"Jasiah?"

I tense, my mother's voice immediately deflating my raging hard-on.

Shit.

I tear my mouth from Sam's then turn to find my parents watching us, a gleeful smile on my mother's face and a smirk on my father's. One I know all too well.

"Hey, guys," I greet them, clearing my throat when I hear how gruff I sound.

"Sweetheart, I didn't know you were coming here tonight," my mom says, quickly moving in for the kill…of my pride that is. I try not to wince when she pulls me down for a kiss, thankfully only one to my cheek and not the thousands she usually gives me.

"Yeah, it was a last minute thing," I tell her. "Sam and I decided to come walk around for a bit."

I'm about to formally introduce them but she strikes first. With her smile bright, she moves to stand in front of Sam. "Hi, sweetheart, I'm Elise Crawford, Jasiah's mother," she says, making me fucking cringe. "It's so nice to meet you."

"Mrs. Crawford, it's nice to meet you, too." Sam shoves the cotton candy against my chest and tries wiping her hands on her skirt. "Sorry, my hands are sticky," she apologizes.

"No problem. I'm a hugger anyway," she says, pulling her into a hug.

"Well good, so am I." Sam returns the embrace, not fazed in the least by my mother's affection.

My mom steps back and introduces my father. "And this is my husband, Ben."

Sam shifts on her feet nervously, her smile faltering. "Hi, Mr. Crawford. Nice to meet you."

"You too, honey." He surprises me by pulling her in for a quick hug, too. Not that I thought he would be rude to her but I didn't think he would be this receptive. "And you can call me Ben."

Sam's smile becomes more relaxed. "All right. Thank you, Ben."

"Isn't she beautiful?" my mom says.

"She is."

Sam's cheeks flush. "Well, thank you. I appreciate the compliment considering I probably have cotton candy all over my face at the moment," she says, sending a playful elbow my way.

"Jasiah, why are you smearing candy on her face?" my mom scolds. "You must have better moves than that."

Sam flashes me an amused smile. "Yeah, *Jasiah*, don't you have better moves than that?"

I grunt. The minute I get her alone, I'll show her those moves by fucking the smirk right off her pretty face.

"Have you guys eaten yet? Want to join us for supper?" my mom asks.

"Oh that's so nice of you to ask. We—"

"I don't think so, Mom," I cut Sam off then feel like a dick when my mom's face falls with disappointment. "It's just because we've been walking and eating as we go but maybe another time."

Thankfully, my dad chooses that moment to step in. "Let them be, Elise. We can do it another time when they have more notice."

"Oh, all right." She pulls me down again but this time by my shirt. "You bring her by the house soon for supper, you hear?"

"I will," I promise her.

"I'll even make your favorite. Chicken parm." She presses a kiss to my cheek then gives it a gentle slap. "Now behave, Jasiah," she says, adding salt to the wound before moving to Sam and enfolding her in another hug. "It was so nice to meet you, sweetheart. We'll have you over to the house soon."

"I'd like that. Thank you."

My dad says his good-bye to her next then gives me a hard clap on the shoulder, a knowing smirk on his face. "We'll see you later, Son. Have a good night."

"Bye." Once they're out of sight, I reluctantly glance at Sam and find her watching me with that smug smile on her face. "Don't fucking say it."

"Jasiah? Your name is Jasiah?"

"No. It's fucking Jase."

"Well I much prefer Jasiah over fucking Jase." She belts out laughing, finding herself hilarious. "You might be an even bigger mama's boy than my brother and that's saying something because—"

I silence whatever else she's about to say with my mouth, thrusting my tongue in and inhaling all of that sassy attitude. It does the trick. She melts against me, a sigh of pleasure leaving her. I back her up against a temporary fence that's been set up for the festival, my hand moving between us to snake up her skirt. Unfortunately, she shoves it away before I reach the sweet spot between her legs.

"Your mother told you to behave yourself, Jasiah," she snickers breathlessly against my lips.

"Well, she's not here right now, *Samantha*…" I trail off when I feel her tense, realizing my mistake too late. Pulling back, I look down at her, my hand moving to the smooth surface of her cheek. "I'm going to get you to like your name if it's the last thing I do."

"I like Sam."

"I do too, but I don't want you to cringe every time you hear Samantha."

"Like you do for Jasiah?" she asks, quirking a brow at me.

"It's not the same thing. You don't like yours because of that asshole, and I'm going to change that."

Her face softens. "And how do you plan to do that?"

My arms encircle her waist before I pick her up off her feet, bringing her face level. "By whispering it when I'm inside of you, buried so fucking deep you will forget every meaningless moment you had with that bastard," I murmur, moving in to brush my lips across hers. "You will forget everyone but me."

She rests her forehead against mine, a soft smile on her pretty face. "I already have. It's hard to remember anyone after having someone like you." The sad note to her voice has my chest pulling so fucking tight it restricts me of breath, the same one she breathes into me whenever she's near.

"Let's get out of here." I want to be alone with her, to get lost in her and pretend she's not leaving me in only a few weeks.

At her nod, I give her one more kiss then place her on her feet and start walking around the back way to skip the crowd. As we pass by a white trailer, Sam jerks me back, her feet rooting in place.

I turn to look at her. "What?"

She points to the trailer next to us, a mischievous smile on her face. "Let's go in there."

Glancing over, I see the logo of a cartoon fortuneteller named Madam Raman. "You can't be serious."

She bites her lip with a giggle. "Why not? It'll be fun. Haven't you ever been curious about this kind of stuff?"

"No. They're a bunch of fucking crooks who rip people off by telling them what they want to hear."

"Humor me anyway, will ya? I've always wanted to see one."

When I make no move to oblige she grips the fabric of my opened button-down shirt and steps into me, bringing her sweet body flush against mine. "Please, for me?"

I relent with a growl, unable to say no to her. "Fine, but after this your ass is mine."

"All yours," she agrees.

Damn straight it is, and tonight I'm going to fucking own it.

"Come on." Smiling excitedly, she takes my hand and drags me around to the front of the trailer where a couple is walking out, the girl giggling hysterically. Probably because she just had the most ridiculous experience of her life.

Once they're out of the way, we climb up the few steps and enter to find a woman sitting at a small round table. She has the biggest hair I've ever seen. It's vibrant red and wrapped with colorful scarves. A thousand bead necklaces adorn her neck that would put any Mardi Gras bitch to shame. If her appearance didn't give her away then all the miniature glass bottles that are lined up on the shelf next to her that are labeled as *love potion* would have done the trick. The only thing this crazy chick is missing is a crystal ball.

"Ah yes, the pretty blonde, come in, come in. I've been expecting you both," she says.

I try not to roll my eyes like a fucking chick and take the seat next to Sam as she sits down at the table.

"I'm not really quite sure how this works," Sam says nervously. "I've never been to one of these before."

"Don't be nervous, honey. I don't bite."

"No, she just takes your money," I grumble under my breath but not low enough.

"A skeptic," she says, not seeming offended by my subtle outburst. "That's all right, handsome. I already knew you would be but you'll see. You all do eventually." She returns her attention back to Sam. "So what are you wanting, sugar? Palm reading? Cards?"

"I'm not really sure. What do you suggest?"

"I do best with palms. Thirty dollars for a reading or fifty if he's getting one, too," she says, jerking her thumb at me. "But Mr. Happy Pants needs to comply otherwise it messes with my juju."

I grunt. Her juju is nothing but bullshit, but I refrain from saying that out loud and instead throw thirty dollars on the table. "Just her."

Sam looks at me. "You're not going to get one, too?"

"You go ahead, baby. I'm good."

"All right," she says, disappointment evident in her voice. "I can pay for it myself."

I intercept her when she reaches for her purse. "It's fine. I got it."

"No, it's not. I'll pay for it myself."

"Don't fight him on it, sugar. You won't win. He's always been this way with you," Madam Juju cuts in, acting like she fucking knows me.

I grunt. "Sorry to bust your bubble, lady, but you're already wrong. We just started dating."

Sam gives me a gentle elbow to the ribs.

"I wasn't talking about this lifetime, so you can put that smug smirk away until I'm finished."

I feel Sam stiffen next to me. "This lifetime?"

"Yep. You two are soul mates and were mated in another life."

You have got to be shitting me.

"Give me your hand, honey. I'll tell you more."

I'll just bet she will.

Sam gives the lady her hand, palm up.

"You have a very old soul," she starts, her finger dragging across Sam's soft palm. "This line here is your lifeline and not just this life but it shows you have lived many."

Sam follows the kook's finger, listening intently.

"You're very close with your family," she continues.

"Yes, I am."

She nods. "You always have been. You lost them when you were a young girl in a previous life. It's one of the reasons you hold them so close to your heart now."

My annoyance turns into anger, hating the way this bitch is striking Sam where I know her emotions run deep.

"You are a strong girl and have overcome a lot. Especially recently," she says. "You have some more tough decisions to make, but follow your heart and it will lead you in the right direction." The lady brings her attention to me. "Give me your hand, grumpy. I'm going to show you something."

"I'm good," I tell her, not bothering to hide my irritation.

"Give—me—your—hand."

When I make no move to obey, Sam looks over at me, her eyes pleading. "Please?"

Letting out an annoyed breath, I place my hand on the table. The lady lifts mine and Sam's together, placing them side by side then turns our palms toward us.

"Now, both of you curl your fingers in, just a little."

I do as she says, curious what bullshit she's going to spew next.

"Do you see it?"

Sam takes a closer look at our hands while I remain where I am, staring at the nut job across from me.

The lady leans over the table and uses her finger to trace the line she showed Sam earlier. Then she continues to mine, connecting the two of them.

Sam gasps.

"You see it now, yes?"

"Oh my gosh, yes. We make the shape of a perfect heart."

"It's the symbol of soul mates."

"Oh, come on." I glance over at Sam to see a look of wonderment on her face. "Tell me you're not buying this bullshit?"

"It is not bullshit," the lady argues. "You two are destined to be together. Sorry, for your luck, sugar," she says, making me grunt as she tosses a sympathetic look Sam's way. "He might be a hothead but he does love you."

I tense, my blood heating at the line she just crossed. "Don't put fucking words into my mouth."

"Jase!" Sam bites out.

"We're getting out of here. I've sat through this ridiculous shit long enough." Jumping to my feet, I pull out her chair.

"You're scared," the lady says. "And it's gonna bite you in the ass if you aren't careful. You are being given a second chance. Don't take it for granted."

"And you are a fake! Enjoy your thirty bucks, lady."

Taking Sam's hand, I get us the hell out of there before I really lose my fucking cool. I weave in and out of the crowd, dragging her behind me as I head for the parking lot.

Once we make it to my truck, Sam rips her hand out of mine.

"What the hell is wrong with you?"

I turn back to find her glaring at me. "Me?"

"Yes, you. You're acting like an asshole."

I stare back at her incredulously. "You just finished listening to that nut job and you think I'm the asshole?"

"I don't understand what you are so bent out of shape about."

"I'm pissed that some phony filled my girl's head with a bunch of bullshit and played on her emotions."

"How do you know it's bullshit? Look what she said about my family, that was accurate."

"It's an easy statement to make. How many fucking people aren't close with their family?"

She crosses her arms. "Fine, then what about the heart symbol?"

"What about it? I'll bet anyone who puts their hands together like that makes the symbol. She's a fake, Sam. You can't possibly think anything she said has merit. She sells love potion for christ's sake."

"Well, too bad she doesn't sell a romance one, I would have bought a bottle and doused you in it!"

I grunt.

"Haven't you felt it, Jase," she whispers, her expression softer. "Like we've done this before? From the first moment you touched me, I swear my heart remembered it. How do you explain that?"

"We have a strong connection. That has never been questioned. That lady over there though"—I point toward the trailer—"her fucking sanity is questionable."

"You don't believe there could be the slightest possibility of past lives?"

"No. I don't. I believe when we die we go to this great place where angels fly around with harps singing halle-fucking-lujah while we all hang out and have a good time. If I'm really lucky they'll all be naked and look just like you."

She doesn't laugh like I hoped she would. Only a sad smile cracks her perfect lips, revealing all the broken pieces of her and igniting a storm of emotions inside of me.

I release a breath. "Look, Sam—"

"Just forget it."

She turns to leave but I don't let her. Snagging her arm, I spin her back around to face me. "Are you seriously mad at me because I don't believe in her bullshit?"

"No. That's not what this is about."

"Then what the fuck is it about?"

It looks like she's about to tell me but then thinks better of it.

"Fine. Let's play this how you really want it to go. Let's say this lady is right. We're soul mates and destined to be together. And...so what? What the fuck does it matter when you're moving away? Does believing her change that?"

It's on the tip of my tongue to tell her I'd believe it all if it meant she would never leave, but I hold back.

She remains silent, tears welling in her sparkling green eyes.

"That's what I thought." I fight like hell against the burning sensation in my chest. "*Now,* we can forget about it." I walk around to my driver's side door only to see Sam walk past my truck, heading out of the parking lot. "Where the hell are you going?"

She turns back around with tears streaming down her cheeks, the sight striking me like a stake to the fucking heart. "Home. I want to be alone right now."

She turns her back on me again, her feet moving faster.

"Sam!"

She doesn't turn back around.

"Fuck!" I slam my hand against my truck before gripping my hair in frustration.

"Lover's quarrel?"

I spin around to find Stephanie sauntering toward me with a smug smile.

"Fuck off, Stephanie. I'm not in the mood for your shit right now," I say, reaching for my door handle.

"You had to know it wasn't going to work out, Jase. She's a stuck-up bitch just like the rest of her family."

I turn back to her, my fingers gripping the door handle so tight my knuckles are white. "Say one word about her again and you'll live to regret it."

She crosses her arms angrily over her chest but there's no denying the way her eyes flare nervously. I'd never hit a chick, but I swear if she fucks with Sam I'll make her pay.

"It's only a matter of time until Sawyer finds out."

The mention of his name has my already hot blood pumping ruthlessly through my veins. A reminder that once again he will eventually take a girl from me. Only this time it's one I actually care about.

"Stay the fuck away from me and stay away from Sam," I say before getting into my truck and driving away.

CHAPTER 15

Sam

I walk downtown, window-shopping as I make my way to Overtime to give Zoey the four thousand dollar check I owe from the auction. It's a big portion of my savings but worth every penny. Not only for the Center but it also bought me time with Jase that we might not have had otherwise.

Tears burn the back of my throat as I think about our fight the other night. It seems so silly now but at the time I was really hurt. What Madam Raman said really resonated with me. I've always felt this pull with Jase that I've never experienced with anyone else. That feeling of déjà vu, but the thought only seemed appalling to him. It hurt to think my feelings are possibly stronger for him than his are for me. But I shouldn't have stormed off the way I did. I've missed him so much these past two days.

My plan was to call him this afternoon but then I remembered he works the night shift this evening, so I figure it's best to wait and call him tomorrow. I pray we can move past it. I just want to go back to how things were before we went and saw Madam Raman.

I shove my turmoil aside as I come up to Overtime, focusing on the here and now. Walking in, I find the place pretty much empty, which I expected since they don't open for another two hours. What I didn't expect was Austin and Zoey in a heated discussion. They stand behind the bar, him crowding her against the liquor cabinet. He's leaned in close, his arms caging her on either side. Zoey glares up at him but there is no denying the flush of her cheeks.

I consider quietly slipping out, not wanting to interrupt, but I don't get the chance before Zoey notices me.

"Sam," she says, surprise clear in her voice. She pushes against Austin's chest. "Move out of my way, you bossy brute."

He makes no effort to comply and instead leans in even closer. "This isn't over, Zoey. I'm not giving up," he murmurs before finally stepping out of her personal space and moving for the door.

"Hey, Austin," I greet him awkwardly, hoping to ease some of the tension.

"Hey, Sam."

"Not working today?" I ask.

"I'm on the night shift and headed there now. I just had to make a stop first," he says, shooting a look Zoey's way.

Her eyes narrow as she gives him a look of her own. The tension is so thick you could cut it with a knife.

"Well, have a good night and be safe," I say.

He nods. "I always am. Take care."

Hearing the door close behind me, I make my way over to Zoey where she sits on one of the bar stools. "What the heck was that about?"

She drops her forehead on the counter with a groan, the resounding thud making me wince. "God, Sam, I'm in serious trouble."

Concern plagues me at the defeated sound of her voice. "Why? What happened?"

She lifts her head, pinning me with her tired eyes. "I slept with him."

"Austin?" I screech, shock coursing through me.

She nods. "Yeah, the night of our date. And let me tell you, it was like nothing I've ever experienced before. Not that I sleep around, but no one—and I mean no one—has ever done to my body what that man did to mine. He corrupted parts of me that I never even knew existed."

I smile, knowing exactly what she's talking about. "Sounds incredible."

"Oh, it was incredible all right. Which is the problem, because it can never happen again."

"Why not? You guys are perfect for each other."

"I can't. I have Chrissy to think about. When I'm not here working my butt off to pay for all the medical bills then I'm with her. I can't let anything interfere with that. I'm all she has."

My heart twists in my chest for both her and Chrissy. I wish she would let my family help her more, but she is so stubborn and refuses any financial assistance from us unless she's really scrambling.

"Zoey, listen, I get it. I really do. You know how much Chrissy means to me as well but you need to have a life, too. She would want that. You can have both."

She shakes her head, tears welling in her eyes, and it hurts me something fierce. Zoey isn't a crier. For all the years I've been friends with her, I've only ever seen her shed a tear a time or two. She is one of the strongest women I know, but as time goes on, the responsibility of her sister is wearing her down.

I pull her in for a hug, squeezing her tight. "Just think about it, please?" I plead before leaning back to look at her. "I'll bet Austin would not only respect your time with Chrissy but also be a part of it."

She gives me a watery smile. "Yeah, maybe."

The *maybe* is halfhearted and doesn't give me much hope, but I don't press, knowing that's not what she needs right now. It will only make her back away more from the idea.

She waves a hand in front of her face before perfecting that mask of hers. "Anyway, enough about me. What's going on with you? How are things with your sexy firefighter?"

I had planned to share with her what happened between Jase and me, wanting advice, but I decide she has enough on her plate right now without adding my problems to it. "Great." The lie flows easily from my lips. "Actually, I came by to bring you this." Reaching into my purse, I pull out the check and hand it to her.

Her brows bunch in confusion. "What's this for?"

"For the auction, silly. Would you mind giving it to the fundraising committee?"

"Sam, Jase already paid for it."

Every muscle in my body stills. "What?" I ask, swearing I misheard her.

"He paid it a few days after the auction. He didn't tell you?"

I shake my head, shock robbing me of words.

"I was pretty surprised myself when he came in," she says, since all I can do is stare at her like an idiot. "When I asked why he was paying for it he said the last person who should ever pay for a date is you."

My heart melts into a giant puddle of goo, tears stinging my eyes.

"It was pretty much the same thing Austin said to me."

"Austin paid for yours, too?" I ask past my burning throat.

She nods. "Yeah, the sweet fucker."

A laugh explodes from me but quickly turns into a sob and now it's me who drops my forehead on the table.

"Sam? What is it? What's wrong," Zoey asks, her hand rubbing soothing circles on my back.

I shake my head, not knowing how to explain what I'm feeling. About Jase and me, about moving, about everything Madam Raman said...

Lifting my head, I look at Zoey and see her eyes dark with concern. "Do me a favor, will you?"

"Of course, anything," she says.

"Give me your hand."

Frowning, she does as I say.

My fingers encircle her wrist as I hold her palm up next to mine. "Curl the tips of your fingers just a bit."

She does but what I thought might happen doesn't. There is no heart, only our lines flowing into one another.

"Uh, Sam? Are you feeling okay?" she asks slowly. Seeming to fear for my mental state.

A smile of contentment spreads across my lips as I continue to stare at our hands. "Yeah. Actually, I'm more than okay."

CHAPTER 16

Jase

"Holy shit, what the fuck?" Declan hollers, jumping back from his locker when he opens it and a naked inflatable chick jumps out at him, hitting him in the face.

Laughter fills the room; Cam's being the loudest since it was his prank.

"Phillips, you asshole," Declan yells, whipping the doll at him.

"Aw, come on, rookie. It's a present from me to you. Look, her mouth is even open, waiting for your cock."

Another round of chuckles fill the room. Playing pranks on rookies is a common thing, we all had to endure it at one point, but Declan gets it the worst since his uncle is the fire chief for the entire division of Colorado.

I, however, don't find today's prank as funny as everyone else but that's because I'm pissed off. It's been two days since I've spoken to her. I miss her like fucking crazy but I have too much pride to apologize first. However, if I don't hear from her soon, I'm caving. I need to be with her. I don't want to waste the rest of our time together fighting. I want to spend it with her—inside of her.

"What's up with you?" Jake asks me as I slam my locker shut, harder than necessary.

"Nothing," I mutter, but we all know I'm lying. These guys are my best friends and know me better than anyone else. Actually, we're more than friends.

Here, we're brothers.

"Trouble in paradise?" Cam asks, earning himself a glare from me. "Thought so." He chuckles.

"Why, what happened?" Austin asks.

I drop down on the bench and let out a heavy breath. "I don't know. We went to the street festival the other night and she wanted to see this psychic. The lady was a fucking nut job." I tell them the whole story, right up until the moment Sam stormed away.

"Soul mates? Past lives?" Jake grunts in disbelief.

"Exactly, it's bullshit."

"So you think Sam's mad because you didn't believe this lady?" Austin asks.

I shrug. "I guess so. She said it wasn't about that but what else could it be?"

"Depends. How much of an asshole were you?" he asks with a smirk.

"I wasn't. Not to her anyway. Only to Madam Juju but she deserved it. You should have seen the way she messed with Sam's head."

It still pisses me off just thinking about it.

"Maybe Sam's upset because you thought it was impossible to love her in another life," Cam says, cutting back in. "Chicks are sensitive like that."

Austin lifts a brow at me. "Never thought about that. He could be right."

"Of course I'm right," he shoots back. "We've talked about this. I know chicks. I know what they want. Why do you think I get laid so much?"

We all grunt, but I think about what he said. Could she be upset about that?

Haven't you felt it, Jase. Like we've done this before? From the first moment you touched me, I swear my heart remembered it. How do you explain that?

Like I said before, we have a connection—a strong one. One I've never had with anyone else. But that doesn't mean that chick is right and even if she were, it wouldn't matter anyway.

"I don't see why she would be mad about that when she's the one leaving in a few weeks," I grumble, speaking my thoughts, which only adds to the restriction in my chest. I've barely survived these past two days without her. How the hell am I supposed to survive when she's gone for good?

"Is she still leaving?" Jake asks.

I shrug. "I guess so."

"What, you guys haven't talked about it?"

"No. I don't like to talk about it because I don't want her to fucking go," I admit for the first time out loud.

"Then tell her that, you idiot," Cam says, making it sound so easy.

I shake my head. "No. I won't do that to her. She wants to be closer to her family, and I won't take that from her."

No matter how much I want to.

"Take it from me, boy, you're better off," the captain says, walking in with a slice of pizza in his hand. "Get a dog. They're much less complicated than women."

Another collection of grunts fill the room. Now this guy has merit when it comes to this shit. He's been married three times. Part of the reason why he's so cynical, I think. Finding a woman who will stay committed to us and our jobs is not easy and he's proof of that.

I could see Sam doing it though—respecting it… *Stop right there, Crawford. It's never going to happen.*

Jesus, I've never been this messed up over a girl before. Of course it had to happen with one who is moving across the fucking country to live next to a guy I hate.

Cap's right. I'm getting a fucking dog.

Before any of us can say more, the tone sounds, alerting us of a call and putting everyone into motion. Dispatch gives us the location as we all rush to gear up.

Attention, Fire Station Two. Two car collision located northeast of Deerbrook Road. One driver possibly intoxicated and one victim trapped inside an overturned vehicle.

The engine roars to life, sirens crying out as we all pile in and move out. Mikey stands at the overhead door, seeing us off before closing up.

That first surge of adrenaline rushes through my veins, this is what we wait for, what we train for.

Cap radios dispatch, stating that we're en route with an ETA of four minutes. Every prior thought is eliminated as we speed through the night. The only thing that matters right now is who is waiting on the other side of this call.

Arriving at the scene we find a Dodge pickup with a dented front end sitting haphazardly in the road. The other car is wedged between a ditch and a light pole, the driver's side a mangled mess.

My gut twists in a dreaded knot for whoever is sitting inside of it.

"A power line's been hit, boys, be cautious," Cap warns us as we come to an abrupt stop near the scene.

A civilian runs up as we jump out, his cell phone in hand. "I'm the one who called it in. He T-boned her," he explains, pointing to the driver of the truck who is stumbling around, blood trickling down his forehead.

"I swear, I didn't see her. She came out of nowhere," he says, driving a nervous hand through his hair.

"He's drunk," the man adds, voice tight.

The information has my own temper sparking. We see this far too often and it never fails to incite a deep-seated anger in me.

The captain begins shouting orders at each of us. Austin and I are told to assess the victim's injuries while the others contain the scene until the police arrive. "Paramedics should be here soon but let's try to get the victim out of that car, now!"

The pungent smell of gasoline assaults my nostrils as we approach, putting me on alert. I bend down to look inside the shattered window and find a young girl hanging upside down, held in place by her seatbelt. Her torso is soaked with blood, a twisted piece of metal piercing her stomach.

Shit.

"Please, help me," she cries weakly.

"That's what I'm here for. Everything is going to be okay." Opening the first aid kit next to me, I drop to my back and wedge myself inside the small hole of the window to get a better look at her injury.

It's not good.

"What's your name, beautiful?" I ask, pulling out my gauze to wrap around the wound, in an attempt to stanch the loss of blood.

"Samantha," she whispers.

Every muscle in my body stills. I peer up into her pale blue eyes, trying not to imagine a pair of emerald ones. "Pretty name for a pretty girl," I say but can hear how gruff my voice sounds. "How old are you, Samantha?"

"Seventeen."

Even younger than I thought.

"My parents are going to be so mad," she cries.

"Nah, they'll be relieved you're okay." I pray like hell I can keep it that way. "Can you feel your legs, Samantha?"

"I can't feel much, I'm so cold," she chatters, her voice weak and sluggish, telling me she's possibly going into shock due to the amount of blood loss.

"Crawford, get out now, the power line is collapsing!" Before I can comprehend Austin's warning, I hear a loud crash then feel a spark of heat.

"Fuck!" Austin bellows.

Dread curls its icy fingers around my heart, robbing me of precious air. I stare up into the young girl's glassy eyes, watching helplessly as blood gurgles from her lips.

"You heard him, Crawford. Out!" the captain yells.

"Please don't leave me," she cries, her voice drowning in her own blood.

"I'm not going anywhere. I promise." Knowing I need to move fast, I quickly reach for my utility knife and begin sawing through her seatbelt.

"Crawford! I said get out! That's a fucking order!"

Ignoring the captain, I continue my task, my hands fucking shaking with urgency as I try to free her. "I'm going to get you out of here, Samantha, but we have to move quickly, okay?"

"'Kay," she complies, her voice barely above a whisper.

"Hawke, help me!"

Austin is already there, dropped down next to my waist. I feel bad putting him in this position, knowing he's deliberately disobeying the captain's orders.

Once I cut through the seatbelt, I carefully bring her down on top of me only to hear her let out a cry of pain.

"Easy, I got you."

Austin drags us out as I hold her close. As we clear the car, I can feel the intense heat and hear the roar of flames.

"Go, go, go!"

Cradling her to my chest, I run in the opposite direction of the car. Once I'm far enough away, I lower her onto the ground and see blood purging past her lips, her breathing labored.

"Stay with me, Samantha." I begin chest compressions but with every pump she fades further from me. "Come on!" I grind out, grief gripping my frantic heart.

I don't stop until the paramedics shove me out of the way, but I remain by her side, not leaving her like I promised. However, there was nothing any of us could do. She died right there on the highway next to me, her young life cut short because of one senseless choice.

"I swear, man, I never saw her. I didn't mean for this to happen."

I twist my head and find the cops talking to the stumbling asshole. It's then I let my emotions get the best of me. Getting to my feet, I run at him, rage pumping viciously through my veins. "You son of a bitch!"

Austin's there to take me down before I have the chance to reach him. "Let it go. It won't bring her back."

Maybe not, but it will make me feel a lot fucking better to make him hurt, have him endure the pain she felt moments before her death.

"Samantha!"

The frantic voice snaps me out of my anger. Both Austin and I crane back to see a lady in her pajamas, running to where Samantha lies lifeless on the ground, but a cop is there to intercept her before she can reach the paramedics.

"Please, let me go. That's my baby."

I watch the cop murmur something to her and realize he's telling her the devastating news.

The most agonizing scream pierces the night air as she drops to her knees. Her cries of devastation are ones that will haunt me for the rest of my life.

Oftentimes, people call us heroes, but we aren't. Not always. Sometimes our best isn't good enough, and for the first time in my career—mine wasn't. I couldn't save her. Now, her blood covers my hands and will stain my soul forever.

CHAPTER 17

Sam

A sound startles me awake. Lying in the quiet dark of my room, I listen. A few moments pass before I hear it again and realize there's someone at my door.

"What on earth?" I mumble and glance at the clock to see it's three in the morning. Concern plagues me as I wonder who it could be since Jase is at work, and even if he wasn't I doubt it would be him. We still haven't spoken since our fight. The reminder has pain slicing through my fragile heart.

I begin to wonder if it's Zoey and if something has happened to Chrissy but surely she would call if she needs me.

Tentatively, I climb out of bed and slip on my silk robe, my tired eyes gritty and raw. I walk out into my living room, keeping my steps quiet. The knock sounds again, louder this time, and elicits a yelp from me.

"Sam, it's me. Open up!"

Jase?

Something in his voice has me moving quickly. Gripping the handle, I look through the peephole just to make sure then swing open the door. The sight I'm met with has my heart squeezing painfully in my chest. Jase stands with his arms braced on the doorframe, his head hanging in defeat. The misery on his handsome face striking me all the way to my soul.

He looks so lost…broken.

"Jase, what is it? What's wrong?" I step closer, my hand finding his strong jaw. The roughness of his damp cheek sends my thundering heart sinking straight to my stomach.

Without a word, his arms come around me and his mouth steals mine in the most devastating kiss I've ever felt. Tears burn the back of my throat, yet, for the first time since our fight, my heart lights up at the feel of his lips against mine.

My arms circle his neck, pulling him in, giving him everything I have, hoping it's enough to take away whatever has him so upset. Picking me up off my feet, he kicks the door closed behind him and carries me into my room.

Seconds later, my back meets the bed, his hard body blanketing mine. He unties my robe, peeling it open before his large hands smooth over the soft surface of my matching satin tank top and shorts, eliciting goose bumps across my skin.

"I need you," he whispers against my lips, his voice guttural.

"You have me. Always."

With urgent hands, we quickly remove each other's clothes, connecting skin-to-skin—soul-to-soul. The moment he enters me, my shattered world feels whole again. Nothing else matters but this—us.

His groan vibrates against my neck where his face is buried. "I missed you so fucking much."

"Me, too. So much." My fingers get lost in the grooves of his back as he moves inside of me with absolute perfection, each stroke more beautifully devastating than the last.

He lifts his face to trail soft kisses across my cheekbone before bringing his lips to my ear. "Samantha," he breathes. "*My* Samantha."

It's not only the possession in his voice that has me completely falling apart, but also the conviction in it. The sob I've been trying to hold back rips from me, the significance of this moment is something I will remember forever.

"Say it, baby."

"Your Samantha," I whisper back, tears spilling down my cheeks.

I am his; I think I always have been, even before I knew it. Which is why I have a very hard decision to make because I can't lose this. Not now and not ever.

After we finish making love, he holds me in the dark, both of us silent. Words are useless right now. Our kisses. Our touches. They said everything that needed to be said.

At least for now.

The sound of his steady heartbeat under my cheek and the warm safety of his arms lull me back to sleep. But just as I slip off, I could have sworn I heard him whisper, "Don't leave me."

CHAPTER 18

Jase

The following morning, I wake up to be greeted by the face of an angel, one that I would give anything to wake up to every morning for the rest of my life.

Yeah…I'm that fucked.

Regret still weighs down on me from the night before, but I can finally breathe again and that's thanks to the girl next to me. She was the only one who could have brought me out from the dark place I was in. She didn't ask questions. She didn't need to know what happened. But she knew exactly what I needed.

And it was her.

Her soft hand rests on the side of my face, thumb stroking my jaw. "Morning," she whispers.

I pull her warm, naked body in closer. "Morning."

"Do you want to talk about last night?"

"Not really," I answer honestly.

I wouldn't know where to start. It was the worst night of my life, definitely of my career. But I know it was not as shitty as that girl's parents'. My chest tightens at the memory of her mother. It turns out she was waiting for Samantha to get home from work but when she was late and didn't pick up she knew something was wrong and tracked her phone.

Sometimes, technology isn't a good thing.

I've been on hundreds of calls but this one meant something more than the others. Her name only added to the blazing anger and regret inside of me but it also opened my eyes to what I have and what I could potentially lose.

I ended up being sent home by one pissed off captain, which is why I came here. I'm praying I didn't fuck up my career. I love my job and respect my captain, but I couldn't walk away from that car without Samantha, even if it meant dying with her. I had to at least try. Unfortunately, in the end, it didn't matter.

Sam places a kiss on my burning chest. "Let me have a shower then we'll talk."

Talk. Yeah, we need to talk. I'm assuming she means about the other night but the conversation weighing heavily on mind is the one where I tell her I can't let her go. I can't lose her. She's the best thing that's ever happened to me and even if we have to do it from hundreds of miles away, I'll do whatever it takes to keep her.

She rolls out of bed, giving me an incredible view of her naked body before she shields it with her soft pink robe. The one I couldn't get off her fast enough last night.

Sitting up, I move to the side of the bed and grab her around the waist before she can walk away, burying my face into her soft stomach.

Her slender fingers sift through my hair. "Are you sure you're okay?"

"Yeah, baby. As long as I have you, I'm good."

Her arms curl around my neck, hugging me back for another few moments before I let her go.

"I'll be fast," she promises, before walking into the bathroom and closing the door behind her.

As the shower turns on, I consider joining her, but before I can make the decision there's a knock on the door. Pulling on my jeans, I swipe my shirt off the floor and walk out of the room. I toss it over my head as I open the door and freeze when I see who's on the other side of it.

Well fuck.

Definitely not someone I expected or want to see for that matter, especially right now.

His shocked expression only lasts a second before his eyes narrow with the same hatred I have brewing inside of me. "So, it's fucking true. My sister's been slumming."

I relax against the doorframe when I feel anything but and say the first hateful thing I can think of. "You had to know payback was going to happen sooner or later, Evans."

I don't get the chance to regret the words before his fist connects with the side of my jaw, pain exploding throughout my head. I strike back, all the anger and resentment that's been built up over the years boils over, drowning us both in nothing but revenge.

Sam

Before I can step into the shower, I turn off the water, thinking I heard a knock on my door. Pulling my robe back on, I walk out of the bathroom. "Jase is that someone at my door?"

"So, it's fucking true. My sister's been slumming."

My feet falter as I make it into the hallway; Sawyer's voice laced with disdain sends my heart plummeting.

Oh god. What's he doing here?

"You had to know payback was going to happen sooner or later, Evans."

I flinch; his words are like a hot iron, painfully striking my soul. I can't find my breath, my knees growing weak.

How could he say that?

I'm knocked out of the painful fog when I see Jase stumble backward, my brother coming at him full force.

"You're fucking dead, Crawford!"

Jase meets him head-on, both of them crashing to the floor in a fit of rage as they match each other blow for blow.

"Both of you, stop it right now!" I run over to where they grapple in front of my kitchen island, their fists striking out hard and fast. "Please stop!" I scream, a sob tearing from me, terrified they're going to kill each other.

I look around for something that will help me break them apart and my eyes land on the sprayer attached to the kitchen sink. Reaching over, I turn on the cold tap water then yank the hose out as far as it will go and squeeze the handle.

Cold water rains down on them both.

"What the fuck?" Sawyer bellows.

It gives me the split-second I need. Moving quickly, I grab Sawyer's shirt and push Jase away at the same time before wedging myself between them, knowing they won't go through me to get to each other.

"What the hell is the matter with you two?" Angry tears threaten to spill over, but I valiantly hold them in as I stare back and forth between two men I love more than anything in this world. One who just deliberately broke my heart. "Sawyer, go into my room," I tell him, but my gaze is focused on Jase who has yet to look me in the eye.

"I'm not fucking going anywhere."

I turn on him, letting him see my pain and anger. "You either go into my room or you leave and never come back."

We both know I'm serious. I don't say things unless I mean them. His jaw tenses but he's smart enough to listen and reluctantly leaves the room, slamming the door behind him.

I refocus my attention back to Jase and watch him wipe blood from his busted lip. "Payback, Jase? Really?" I grind out, my heart cracking as I repeat the hurtful words.

"I didn't mean it," he says, his breathing harsh and angry. But he still refuses to look at me, keeping his eyes trained on the floor.

"Then why did you say it?" I snap.

His eyes finally lift to mine, and while I see regret, I also find so much anger. "Because I fucking hate him, and I always will. That's never going to change, Sam!"

His words rip through my already wounded heart, ending what

could have been a beautiful future. It was only minutes ago I had made the decision to stay because I loved him too much to leave, but it doesn't matter. Not anymore. He will never let go of this vendetta against my brother, someone who has the same blood as me running through his veins.

"I hate you too, asshole!" Sawyer yells from the other end of the door.

Shaking my head, I swallow past my burning throat. "Get out."

"Sam…" he starts but trails off.

"I said get out!"

His eyes hold mine, pleading yet resolved before he finally moves for the door. "I'm sorry. I never meant to hurt you."

I look away, unable to watch him walk out of my life forever. The sound of the door closing drives the final nail into my mangled heart. I cover my mouth with both hands, trying to breathe through the excruciating pain in my chest.

I hear the click of my bedroom door and feel my brother's presence. With a blurry gaze, I look up into his green eyes, the same color as mine, and see so much betrayal in them, adding to all the emotions suffocating me.

"How did you find out?" I ask.

"Anonymous phone call." His voice is tight, sounding as angry as he looks.

I shake my head, having a pretty damn good idea who it was.

That meddling bitch.

"It's not what you think."

"Oh, I think it is," he says. "My own sister sleeping with the fucking enemy."

My head snaps back up, fury overriding my pain. "This isn't about you, Sawyer!"

"How the fuck can you say that? This has everything to do with me."

"No, it doesn't. This is about me and my feelings. What I had with him has nothing to do with you!" I scream back but my anger quickly turns to devastation. "I love him, and I thought he loved me." The sob I've been holding in finally breaks free. It tumbles past my lips and is so painful it steals my breath.

Sawyer's hard expression softens. With a heated curse he moves closer, wrapping me in his protective arms as I sob on his shoulder, tears of pain and agony soaking his shirt.

"Come home, Sam," he murmurs against the top of my head. "We'll take care of you."

Home.

Something I thought I finally found with Jase, but I was wrong. The thought has me crying harder. There's nothing left for me here.

Not anymore.

CHAPTER 19

Jase

With a black eye and swollen jaw, I sit across from my captain, who still looks as pissed as he did when he sent me home the other night.

"You're a fucking mess," he states, as if I didn't already know this.

My entire world is in fucking shambles. I just lost the only girl I'll ever love all because I let my anger run my mouth, and now I'm probably going to lose the career I've spent my life working for.

He doesn't elaborate further on my battered face and cuts right to the chase. "What the hell were you thinking disobeying orders the other night?"

"I'm sorry," I offer the apology but it's weak.

"Are you?"

Silence hangs heavy in the air, the lie dangling in the back of my throat, but I can't do it. "No. I'm not. And I'm going to be honest and tell you that I would do it again."

"The hell you will! You know the rules, Crawford."

"Fuck the rules!" I snap. "At what cost do we follow those rules, Cap? Don't tell me you wouldn't have done the same thing as me. You wouldn't have left her in that fucking car and we both know it."

He eases off, resting back into his chair. "Maybe not, but it doesn't mean it's the right decision. You put yourself and Hawke in danger when you knew she wasn't going to make it."

"Yeah, but at least I did everything I could." I shake my head, trying to ward off the memories. "I'll never forget the look on her face. For as long as I live that image will haunt me. If I had left her there then I would have never known and her blood would be on me. I couldn't live with that, Cap. I'd rather die with her."

He stares back at me, his expression somber. "Listen, I don't want anyone dying on my watch either but sometimes, even despite our best efforts, we can't save them all. You made a reckless decision and not only put yourself at risk but Hawke, too. We want to save lives but not at the cost of our own. You cannot help anyone if you're dead."

"You're right," I agree, looking at it from his perspective. "Let's hope that from now on my best will be good enough to keep everyone alive. That is, if you let me keep my job."

I brace myself, fearing for his answer. Losing this job would be one more blow I couldn't live with right now.

"Of course I'm going to let you stay. You and those dipshit friends of yours are the best I have," he says, making me smirk. "But you will follow orders when I give them and you're taking time off."

"I don't need it. I'm good."

"The hell you are. Don't start lying to me now, Crawford. You're a mess and you damn well know it."

I blow out a heavy breath. "I need to work right now, Cap. I need the distraction."

"It's not up for discussion. Take the time and work out whatever you need to with that girl of yours. I don't want you back here until your head is on straight."

"I don't have a girl anymore. That's why I want to keep working," I tell him, my teeth grinding at the pain infiltrating my chest.

"Why the hell not?"

I remain silent, not in the mood to talk about it right now...or ever.

"Look, I'm going to tell you something that I wish someone would have told me. But if you breathe a word of it to anyone, I will deny it. Got it?"

I nod, my curiosity piqued.

"I know I always tell you guys to forget about women and get a dog.

Now sometimes that is the way to go. But other times…it's not. Some women are worth the headache, believe me, I know. I had one and I fucked it up," he says, surprising me. "Now I may not know that girl well—hell, I only met her a couple of times—but everyone knows your arrogant ass won't ever find better than her."

That's because there is no one out there better than her.

"If you let her go, you'll end up a cynical asshole like me and marry all the wrong ones. Trust me. You don't want that."

I let his words sink in, wondering if it's that easy. I'm worried I fucked up too bad for her to forgive me this time. But I have to at least try, I can't survive without her and no damn dog will do.

A newfound hope flares inside of me, pushing me to my feet. "Thanks, Cap."

I extend my hand to him and he returns the gesture with a firm handshake. "You're welcome. Now get out of here and go grovel your ass off. And take her flowers. It'll help."

"Jesus, you sound like my mother."

He grunts. "Remember, tell anyone and I'll deny it."

"Don't worry. Not a word," I promise with a smirk.

Leaving his office, I head out of the station when Cam comes running out after me. "Crawford, wait up."

Shit!

I turn back to him, expecting an earful for avoiding his and everyone else's calls, something I don't really have time to listen to right now.

"What the fuck happened? We've been trying to call you."

"I know. I'm sorry. Listen, I'll explain everything later. I can't talk right now. I have to see Sam."

"Well, you better hope she's still there."

My swift feet falter. "What the hell are you talking about?"

"I saw Evans last night. He said he was taking Sam home with him today."

Panic strikes me hard and fast, making blood rush in my ears. "What?" I choke out, praying I misheard him.

"That's why we've been trying to call you."

"When?"

"I don't know. He just said today, but—"

I don't waste time to hear the rest and haul ass to my truck at breakneck speed. With a heavy foot, I race to her apartment, arriving in half the time it should have taken me to get here.

My feet pound the pavement, urgency propelling my every step as I run into the building, slipping past a couple as they walk out. I forgo the elevator and run up the stairs, knowing it will be faster.

As soon as I reach her door, I rap on it with a heavy fist. "Sam, baby. It's me. Open up."

When I get nothing, I try the handle but find it locked. I'm about to break it down when an elderly neighbor sticks her head out. "Sorry, honey, you missed her. She already left."

Dread grips my chest, stealing every bit of precious air around me. "How long ago?" I ask, hoping to catch them at the airport, refusing to give up.

She can't be gone.

"Her and that handsome brother of hers left early this morning. The movers are set to come tomorrow. I promised her I would let them in," she explains with a smile, having no idea that my entire world just fell out from under me. "You wouldn't happen to be Jase, would you?"

I nod, unable to find my voice from the grief suffocating me.

"One second. I have something for you," she says before disappearing back inside.

I stand a little straighter, a renewed hope igniting in my chest.

She returns a moment later with a sealed envelope addressed to me. "She wasn't sure if you would come by but asked me to give this to you if you did. If you didn't then I was to mail it to you."

"Thanks," I respond, my voice gruff.

Once she retreats back inside, I open the envelope and pull out a folded letter along with a four thousand dollar check.

Jase,

You'll never know how sorry I am that this is being said in a letter, but I worry if I had faced you I wouldn't be able to say what needs to be said.

If I'm being honest, the entire time we were together I never really thought of us as temporary and had prayed for a different outcome. The truth is, I fell madly in love with you.

In a perfect world, you and my brother would be able to make amends because you both love me more than you hate each other, but I now realize that will never happen, and I have to accept that. This isn't about choosing one or the other, I could never do that, but I can't be with someone who hates the people I love. No matter how deep my love runs for you, that vengeance would have eventually broke my heart.

It already has.

I want you to accept this money. The bidding war between bicycle bitch and me is not your responsibility and it was the best four thousand dollars I ever spent. For the Children's Miracle Center but, more than anything, for the time it bought me with you.

I will never forget a second of my time with you. I only wish Madam Raman or whom you like to call "Madam Juju" was right and we could have had eternity.

Take care and be safe, especially when you are fighting fires and jumping off mountains.

Love always,
Sam, Sensible Sam, Crazy Sam, Peaches, and…Samantha.

Sweat drips down my face, mixing with burning regret as I continue my fast glides and take another slap shot.

Living in a hockey town where we get ice year round is definitely a perk. The rink is the only place I want to be at the moment. It's been my second home for most of my life. Here, I can lose myself and travel back to a time when nothing mattered but being with my team and winning. It's a hell of a lot better than drowning my sorrows away in a bottle of Jack. However, the thought is more appealing by the second, anything to ease the burning sensation in my chest.

I have no idea how long I've been here. Right now, I want time to be nothing more than an afterthought, just like the sweet memories of the girl who left her mark on me.

The same one I lost because I'm a fuckup. I've done a lot of stupid shit in my life but losing her has to be the dumbest yet.

Skating along the boards, I glide behind the net before curving around it and flipping the puck up in the top right corner with a wrist shot.

A single applause draws my attention over to the box, and I find my dad leaning against the boards, watching me. The image brings me back to my childhood when he used to coach my team.

Skating over to him, I step through the open gate before dropping down on the bench and grabbing my water bottle. I squirt the cool liquid down my parched throat before soaking my face with it.

"How did you know I was here?" I ask, my breathing heavy from exertion.

"Joe called me, said you've been here for hours," he says, talking about the rink attendant who has worked here longer than I've been alive. "He also said you were sporting quite the shiner." He leans down to get a better look. "I see he wasn't bullshitting."

Yeah, and it still hurts like a son of a bitch. That bastard has a hell of a right hook. But the pain doesn't compare to the one in my chest.

"So you two finally had it out, huh?"

I glance over at him, wondering how he knew it was with Sawyer.

"Cam might have called me, too," he admits, sitting next to me.

Figures. The meddling bastard.

"So, who won?"

I shrug. "I haven't seen what his face looks like, but considering Sam left with him I'd say I lost."

A long moment of silence stretches between us, and I feel his eyes burning into the side of my face but keep my gaze trained ahead.

"You aren't going to fight for her?"

"There's nothing to fight for. She moved to a different state and isn't coming back." Saying the words out loud has the burning pain in my chest spreading throughout my entire body.

"So, you're going to give up. Just like that?"

"I don't have much of a choice."

"You always have a choice, Jase."

I shake my head. "No. Not this time. Even if I were to fight for her, I won't ask her to move back here. She wants to be closer to her family, and I won't take that from her."

"Then don't ask her to."

I finally meet his gaze, my brows furrowing in annoyance. "What, are you saying I should move there?" Not that I didn't entertain the idea at one point but that was before she left without so much as a good-bye. Something that I can't really blame her for. I wouldn't say good-bye to me either.

"Do you love her?" Before I can respond, he holds his hand up to ward me off. "Think long and hard before you answer that. I'm not asking you if you care about her. I'm asking you if you're in love with her. There's a difference. Would you die for her? Would you do anything to make her happy?"

It's an answer I don't need to think about because I've always known it. "Yeah. I love her. I'm pretty sure I loved her before I even knew her." I don't give a shit how ridiculous it sounds; it's the truth.

He nods. "Then don't let her go, Son. Give her the world. Do anything to make her happy, and that includes ending this rival with her brother. Something that I know is probably more John's and my fault than anything. I guess our own feelings bled onto you boys."

My brow lifts in surprise. "Are you saying you were wrong about him?"

"Hell no. He's an arrogant prick," he says. "But I'll respect him because if you love his daughter then I do, too... After all, us Crawfords only pick the best because we are the best."

I smirk but sober quickly as I think the idea over. It would suck to leave my friends, family, and the only home I've ever known but not nearly as much as the thought of never seeing her again. That sucks a whole lot more.

As much as Cap would hate for me to go, I know he would help me relocate to a station nearby. And the guys will understand because they know Sam is worth it. That only leaves one person...

"I doubt Mom will be okay with this," I say.

"Don't worry about her. It'll be tough at first but I'll be there to take care of her. You'll come back to visit and we'll come there."

I grunt. *I wouldn't be surprised if she made him pick up and move, too.*

"Trust me, Son, she'll understand because she knows I would do the same for her. I'd give her anything to make her happy and she expects nothing less from you."

I nod, knowing he's right.

"So, what are you going to do?" he asks. "Are you going to fight or give up?"

I meet his gaze once again, resolution burning my veins. "Fight."

And I won't stop until I win.

CHAPTER 20

Sam

I'm proof that it's possible to live with a broken heart. To continue your day-to-day tasks and keep pushing through, even if you are only taking in half the life and half the breath.

I've been doing it the last four days, but the way my heart yearns you would think it's been an eternity. Each morning I wake up, hoping some of the shattered pieces of my soul will have mended, but they haven't.

I fear I may never be whole again, not without the man who completes me.

I sort through the last box in my bedroom while my mom organizes my kitchen. As if my thoughts summoned it, I find the bangle bracelet with a single peach charm. My heart stutters as I pick it up and slip it on my wrist.

This is the nicest thing anyone has done for me in a really long time, Jase.

Well, that's sad, Peaches. You deserve things like this every day.

A steel vise grips my broken heart and the tears I've managed to keep at bay for today unleash with a vengeance.

"Sam, honey, where do you want…" my mom trails off, coming to a quick stop just inside my room.

I look up at her with tears rushing down my cheeks, not bothering to hide them. I need her too much right now.

"Oh, Sammy." The sadness in her voice mirrors the agony gripping my chest. Dropping whatever she has in her hand, she rushes over and takes me in her arms. "Honey, talk to me. Seeing you so sad these past few days is breaking my heart."

"I miss him so much," I cry, barely managing the words through my broken sobs.

"Who, sweetheart? Grant?"

I try not to cringe, remembering she has no idea about the past couple of months. "No. Jase Crawford."

She stiffens in surprise before pulling back to look at me.

"There's so much I haven't told you, Mom."

Her expression softens. "Then tell me now. Please, Sam. Let me be here for you."

I nod, knowing it's time, and start from the beginning. I tell her everything about Grant and the volatile relationship we had and hold nothing back, not even the abuse.

"No, Samantha." She covers her mouth, muffling the sob of despair that tumbles from her when I tell her about the first time he hit me.

"I'm so sorry."

She pulls me in close again, her comforting arms holding my broken pieces together. "Don't be sorry. I'm the one who is sorry. I should have listened to your father. He knew something wasn't right. I just…I never thought you would keep that from us let alone stay with someone like that."

Shame and humiliation mixes with the burning regret. "Me either," I admit quietly. "But he was good, Mom. He always knew what to say and where to strike. I guess my own insecurities went deeper than I thought."

She looks down at me, tears of devastation staining her cheeks. "What could you possibly feel insecure about?"

I swallow thickly, unsure of how to tell her without sounding jealous or petty, but I try my best and tell her how I've always felt compared to Jesse and Sawyer. "Don't get me wrong, I love them and I love how bright they shine. I just wish I could be more like that, too."

"Oh, Sam." Her slender hands frame my wet cheeks. "You listen to me. You have the most beautiful soul out of anyone I've ever known. You feel things differently than your siblings, you always have, but that is not a weakness. That is your strength. It's who you are," she says, putting it into a different perspective for me. "If I could keep all my babies under one roof I would, but Jesse and Sawyer would never have it," she adds, a soft smile touching her sad lips. "So I keep them close to my heart. But you, Sammy, you let me keep you in my arms and you'll never know how much that means to me. The last several months without you have been torture. I've missed you so much. We all have."

"I missed you guys, too," I cry.

She holds me close, running a comforting hand down my hair, something I've always loved. "Tell me about Jase."

Just hearing his name has my heart breaking all over again. Pulling back, I swipe at my flowing tears then take a deep breath and begin the story of our journey that ended much too soon, starting with the night he stepped in to help me and broke Grant's face.

"Good. That bastard deserves a hell of a lot more," she seethes, some of her pain switching to anger now.

I nod but continue on, not wanting to focus on Grant anymore and share all the moments with her that I had with Jase. From the date auction, to our paragliding experience, and even my idiotic move of getting stuck in the peach tree. Something we both share a laugh over.

"He's incredible, Mom, so much more than I knew. He made me feel things I've never felt, things I didn't know I was capable of feeling."

"You're in love with him," she says with a soft smile.

"Yeah, but it feels so much more than that. If I didn't know better I'd swear I loved him in another life," I admit, thinking about Madam Raman.

"Maybe you did."

Her response takes me by surprise. "You believe in past lives?"

She shrugs. "Honestly, I'm not sure. I believe in God and heaven but there are many things we don't know, Sam. Things that can't be explained but can be felt. When you love someone so much, your heart never forgets it. I know I'll never forget your father, no matter how many lives I live or how much time passes."

I smile, knowing it's true. "What you and Daddy have, I had it with Jase," I tell her quietly. "I know I did. I'll never love someone else like I do him."

She tucks a strand of hair behind my ear, her smile fading. "What happened?"

"Sawyer showed up."

"Oh dear," she sighs. "I guess that's where the black eye came from, huh?"

I nod, pain lancing through me at the memory of their fists striking each other. "It was both of their faults. They said some really hurtful things."

"Oh, I have no doubt Sawyer played a part in it. That boy's mouth runs his common sense sometimes."

"I guess I should have known it would happen eventually but..." I trail off, shaking my head.

"What?" she asks.

"They hate each other so much, Mom," I whisper. "And let's not forget Dad and Mr. Crawford can't stand each other either. Jase and I were doomed from the beginning."

She expels a soft breath, her hand covering mine. "Do you want to know the real reason why your dad and Mr. Crawford don't get along?"

My eyes snap to hers in surprise. "You mean there's a reason behind all of this?"

She hesitates. "More like a past than a reason."

"Please tell me," I plead, needing to know what started this all.

"It goes back to high school. Both your dad and Ben were the epitome of what you would call the school heartthrobs," she says, using her fingers as quotation marks. "They were both arrogant jocks who always had a competitive nature but for the most part they got along. Until they fell for the same girl."

My lips part on a shocked gasp. "No way!"

She nods. "They fought hard to gain her attention, always trying to one-up each other. The hardest part of it all was she liked them both."

It doesn't take long before realization dawns on me. "Oh my god, it was you."

A sad smile cracks her lips. "Yeah. Something I still feel so unworthy for," she admits softly.

"I can't believe it. You and Mr. Crawford." I shake my head, still not believing any of this.

"It wasn't much. I think we went on all of two dates. Ben was your typical tall, dark, and handsome. He could charm a girl with the best of them."

"Just like his son," I say with a smile.

"Yep. Jase is a spitting image of him, just like Sawyer is of your father."

Fathers and sons who are so much alike it's frightening. "I guess we know how it turned out, huh?"

She nods. "I cared about Ben, but I was in love with your father. He was my missing piece. And as bad as I felt for hurting Ben, I will never regret my decision. It was the right one. For all of us."

For obvious reasons, I'm happy she chose my father, too. "Do you think Mr. Crawford still has feelings for you and that's why he and Dad have so much hostility toward each other?" I ask. Though, as I say the words, that doesn't feel right.

"Oh, heavens no. Trust me, it's not that. Ben loves Elise a heck of a lot more than he ever cared about me. You can see it in the way he looks at her."

I agree with that. Even though I was only around them for a few minutes that night, it was very clear to see how much they love each other.

"This has to do with competition and nothing more. Your father hates that Ben had feelings for me and Ben hates that your father won. It angers me that they still hold this ridiculous grudge and it rubbed off on our boys. I have no doubt that the feelings between Sawyer and Jase are because of them."

"It may have started with them but it definitely didn't end with them. Stephanie did that," I grind out, my blood heating at the thought of her, especially after finding out that she was the one who called Sawyer. She's constantly starting shit.

A look of distaste twists my mother's face. "If I could slap the shit out of your brother for that, I would. Jase or not, it was a dumb move."

"I agree with that," I say, but have to admit it was a blessing for Jase whether he thought so at the time or not. "I guess I can understand the competitive nature they all have. I did, after all, fork out four thousand dollars just to beat that bitch."

My mom bursts out laughing, her arm slinging around my shoulders as she pulls me in close. "Ah yes, you come by it honestly, my dear. This family hates to lose, but more than anything, we fight for what we want," she says, her laughter softening into a smile. "And by the sounds of it, you more than got your money's worth."

"Yeah, I did," I admit quietly, my heart growing heavy.

"Call him, Sammy. Talk to him."

I shake my head. "I can't, Mom. He made his feelings perfectly clear. I can't be with someone who hates my brother so much."

"Give him a chance. There's a lot of history that won't go away overnight but I bet, if given half the chance, they'll do it for you."

I remain silent, feeling uncertain. She didn't see the way they attacked each other.

"Just think about it, honey," she says. "Follow your heart, and it will lead you in the right direction."

The problem is, my heart selfishly wants it all—him and my family—but deep down I know it's not possible. So now I'm left with making a choice I'm not sure I can make.

CHAPTER 21

Jase

I park in front of the white and black two-story home and check to make sure I have the right address before climbing out of my rental truck.

Instantly, I'm hit with a heat wave.

Jesus, I've never felt sun like this and the humidity doesn't help. We get hot summers but not like this, this heat is damn near suffocating.

As I head up the porch steps, the front door opens and out steps Mrs. Evans, wearing a floppy sun hat and carrying a watering can.

She falters at the sight of me, her eyes flaring in surprise. "Jase!"

"Mrs. Evans," I greet her with a nod. "I'm sorry to show up unannounced like this, but I was hoping I could speak with you and Mr. Evans for a few minutes. If he's around that is…"

She stares at me for a few more seconds before some of the shock begins to wear off. "Of course, please come in." She steps back inside and holds the door open for me.

"Thanks." I'm thankful for the blast of cold air that greets me as I enter. "I guess air conditioning is a must down here," I remark, trying to break some of the awkward tension.

She smiles, one that reminds me so much of her daughter's. It's easy to see who Sam takes after in the family. "The heat is definitely different in the South but you tend to get used to it."

Good to know.

She eyes me for a moment, something flashing in her soft green eyes just before she reaches up and grasps my chin, turning my face to the side. "You look as bad as my son."

As ashamed as I should feel right now, I can't deny how happy I am to know that fucker didn't walk away unscathed either.

"I'm pretty sure it's even the same eye," she adds, studying my faded bruising.

"Huh. What a coincidence."

Her smile indicates she knows I'm full of shit, but thankfully, she doesn't call me out on it. "Let me get John. He's in his study. Can I get you something to drink while you wait?"

"I'm okay, thanks though."

She gestures over to the living room. "Go on and have a seat. We'll join you in a moment."

Removing my shoes, I head over and take a seat on the plush leather couch. I take in the formal sitting area and pick up a family photo that sits on the end table next to me, my eyes immediately drawing to the girl I've missed so fucking much this past week. Her sparkling green irises and bright smile penetrating my chest as if she were standing right in front of me.

I'm not sure how much time has passed before I hear someone clear their throat.

"Shit!" The picture slips from my hands but I catch it before it hits the ground and place it back on the table. Standing, I turn and face my father's sworn enemy, the same man who also happens to be the father of *my* enemy and the girl I love.

The last one is the only one that matters.

"Mr. Evans," I greet him, extending my hand.

"Jase." He accepts my gesture with a firm handshake but his expression remains somber.

"Why don't we sit down," Mrs. Evans says, taking her husband's hand before bringing him down on the love seat next to her. "Are you sure I can't get you anything, Jase? Coffee? Soda?"

"I'm okay but thanks." An awkward silence fills the room as I sit across from them. "I'm sure you guys are wondering why I'm here."

"I think I might have an idea," she answers with a soft smile, though there's no denying the flash of sadness that suddenly enters her eyes. "I had a big talk with my daughter yesterday. She filled me in on a lot of things…including Grant."

"She did?" I ask in surprise.

She nods. By the pain that washes over her expression, I assume she really does know everything about that bastard. "To be honest, I'm still trying to wrap my head around it," she whispers, her chin quivering as she fights to hold in the tears shining in her eyes. "My heart is having a hard time understanding how someone could hurt her like that." Her breath hitches. "It kills me to know she was so alone." The last of her words fall on a sob, hitting me like a punch to the chest.

John wraps an arm around her and pulls her in close, his expression depicting the same anger I feel.

"She wasn't alone. She had me," I tell her quietly, my own voice gruff and raw.

She gives me a weak smile. "She told me. Thank you for stepping in and helping her. I'd hate to think what would have happened that night had you not shown up."

"No need to thank me. I just wish I could have gotten there sooner. He deserves a hell of a lot more than what he got."

John's furious gaze snaps to mine, his eyes blazing with anger. "It's not over. That son of a bitch is going to pay for touching her."

His fury is something I can relate to. It ignites inside of me every time I think about that bastard striking her.

Sniffling, Catherine swipes at her tears. "What you did for her means a lot to us, and I know the past couple of months has meant a lot to Sam as well."

Her final words instill some hope in me once more. "They've meant a lot to me, too. Which is why I'm here." I pause, not knowing how to start. In the end, I decide it's best to just come right out and say it. "I'm in love with your daughter, and I plan to ask her to marry me."

Catherine's eyes widen in shock while John's narrow. "Marriage," he says, his disapproval evident. "Don't you think it's a little soon for that?"

"I know it may seem that way, sir, but time has no bearing when it comes to what Sam and I have together," I tell him honestly. "When you know, you know. And I know I will never love anyone as much as I love her."

By the smile that takes over Catherine's face, it was clearly the right thing to say. Her husband, however, still doesn't seem convinced.

"Listen, Jase. I appreciate everything you've done for my daughter but..." He shakes his head. "We just got her back and after everything that has happened she needs to be close to her family. I don't think it's a good idea for her to go anywhere right now."

"I have no intention of taking her anywhere. I've been granted a transfer to the Charleston Fire Department and start in two weeks."

Catherine gasps in surprise. "You're moving here?"

"Hopefully. That will be up to Sam."

They continue to stare at me, speechless.

I blow out a heavy breath, realizing this isn't turning out the way I had hoped. "Look. I've made mistakes but I love your daughter, and I'll do anything to make her happy. I'm just asking you to let me be a part of her life, too."

"Oh, Jase." Catherine stands, tears streaming down her face again. I push to my feet as she walks over to me and am surprised when her arms wrap around my waist. "This means so much to me, and I know it will to Sam, too."

"I hope so, but I know having support from the both of you will mean even more."

"Well, you have mine," she says, lifting some of the weight off my chest. She looks over at her husband who still doesn't seem keen on the idea. "He gave up everything for her, John. He loves her."

Silence fills the room, his blank expression making me more nervous by the second.

"What if I say no?"

I debate for only a second about how to answer that before settling on the truth. "I'll ask her anyway."

He grunts but thankfully doesn't knock me out for being honest. "It's not just me you have to worry about. There's my son, too. Sammy cares what he thinks."

I nod. "I know, and I plan to do my part. I get that there's some bad history between our families, but with all do respect, sir, that has no bearing on how I feel about your daughter. And for Sam's sake, I hope we can move past it because I plan to fight for her, no matter what."

"Good boy," Catherine praises, giving my waist an encouraging squeeze.

"I guess Ben and I are to blame for a lot of this," he mumbles. "And it helps that you smashed that bastard's face in."

"I will smash in anyone's face that hurts her, including mine," I tell him, praying it sways his decision.

Smirking, he finally gives me the approval I seek. "Ah hell, as long as you treat her good then you have no problems with me."

The breath I've been holding in since I showed up here releases on a heavy exhale. "Thank you, sir. I promise to take good care of her."

"Don't thank me yet. You still have my son to deal with and he's not going to crack as easily."

"I guess we'll see, I'm headed over there next."

"Oh dear," Catherine breathes nervously. "Maybe you ought to go with him, John."

"No." I dismiss the suggestion right away. "No disrespect, Mrs. Evans, but this is something Sawyer and I need to do on our own."

She sighs. "Fine, but you boys better keep your cool. No fighting in front of my grandbabies."

"No fighting," I promise, hoping it's one I can keep.

"I know my son can be a hothead. He comes by it honestly," she says, shooting a look John's way. "But he loves his sisters very much, especially Sam, and he wants her to be happy, like the rest of us. You tell him what you just told us and I'm sure things will work out."

I wouldn't be so sure of that, but I'm going to damn well try, even if it kills me.

"Beware though, his house is stocked full of guns," John adds with a smirk.

Fucking great!

Letting go of a grudge I've had for so long might be one of the hardest things I've ever had to do. I've been trying to recall when it all started between Evans and me but can't nail down an exact moment. There isn't a time I can remember ever liking him. We've always butted heads, on and off the ice.

It made me realize that maybe the history between our fathers really did play a significant role in our own rivalry. However, it didn't end with them. The moment he fucked Stephanie he took it to a whole new level. It has nothing to do with her because, if I'm being honest, it's not like I ever planned a future with her. Far from it. She was just someone I killed time with. Time that I regret and always will. But him fucking her had everything to do with me. He saw an opportunity to one-up me and he crossed a line. It still pisses me off when I think about it but I've made the decision to get over it.

Stephanie wasn't worth fighting over but Sam is, and I plan to fight until the very end.

I turn off the gravel road and head down the long, paved driveway leading up to his Victorian house in the country and park next to a black Escalade. Knowing this is going to be even harder than what I just did with Sam's parents, I swallow every bit of pride I have and exit the truck.

Grace tentatively steps out of the house as I approach, clearly expecting my arrival. She stands at the top of her porch, wearing a soft pink apron over a yellow sundress, twisting a dishtowel nervously in her hands.

"Sweetness, it's been a long time," I greet her, deciding to break the ice first.

"I see you haven't changed one bit, Jase Crawford."

"Of course not. Why would I change perfection?"

She shakes her head but there's no denying the small smirk that curls the edge of her lips. It quickly softens though, her expression becoming somber as she descends the steps to stand in front of me. "My kids are home. I don't want any trouble here."

"Who said anything about trouble?"

"Yours and my husband's battered faces prove you are both nothing but trouble."

I shrug. "He hit me first."

A bitter laugh escapes her, but there's no amusement behind it. I decide to cut the shit, feeling bad for how anxious she looks.

"Listen, Grace. I'm not here to cause problems. I swear. I'm trying to put an end to this once and for all."

She watches me, still hesitant.

"I'm in love with her. I'm here for her…that's all."

She sighs. "All right. Go on and have a seat on the porch. I'm going to go have the same discussion with my husband. I'll bring ya out some sweet tea in a minute."

"Sounds good, sweetness."

"Jase," she growls, slapping me with her dishtowel. "Cut the sweetness and go sit your ass down now," she orders, pointing to the wicker chairs on the porch.

I chuckle but do as she says, not wanting to piss her off more. I'm going to need her if things don't go well. "You're not going to send my sweet tea out with your husband, are you?" I ask, taking a seat.

She frowns. "No. Why?"

"Because I don't need that shit poisoned. That's why."

I wouldn't put it past the asshole.

No. Not asshole. He is not an asshole. He is the brother of the girl I love.

She smirks. "No. My daughter will bring it out to you. Be good and

I might even give you a slice of pie, too."

"I'm always good."

Her scoff has me chuckling as she heads back inside.

Minutes pass as I sit in the sweltering heat under a ceiling fan that offers little breeze before I hear the creak of the screen door. Looking over, I watch two kids walk out. The little girl looks exactly like her mom but has the same green eyes as her dad and aunt. And a boy who looks exactly like his father but is way cuter…in my opinion.

Before I'm able to introduce myself, the little girl puts down the slice of pie on the table and extends her hand to me. "Hello, Mr. Jase, my name is Hope Catherine Evans and this here is my twin brother, Parker," she says, jerking her thumb over at the boy next to her who holds my glass of sweet tea.

Feeling the first genuine smile I've had since coming here, I take her soft little hand in mine. "Well, it's nice to meet you, Hope Catherine Evans. And you, Parker," I add, although he doesn't seem as receptive as his sister. "I've heard a lot about you two from your Aunt Sam."

"Really?" she asks excitedly. "What did she say?"

"She told me that you and your mom make the best pies in the world."

She smiles proudly, nodding her head. "It's true. Mama and I create the best ones, especially together."

Her not-so-modest answer has me grinning even bigger.

She's my kind of girl.

"Did you make the one I'm about to eat now?" I ask.

"Yes, sir."

"What's this one called?"

Her smile falters and she cuts a glance over at her brother before looking back at me. "Well…" she starts nervously, twisting her tiny hands together in front of her. "Daddy told me to tell you it's called Asshole Pie but then Mama got upset with him and told me to tell you the truth. So it's actually called Sweet Strawberry Pie."

I smirk, amused by her honesty. "I like yours and your mom's name much better." My attention moves to Parker next, and I find him watching me. "How about you, Parker? Your aunt Sam tells me you're quite the hockey player."

He shrugs. "Yeah. So?"

Obviously, he's not as easy to win over as his sister, but I ignore the attitude since I'm sure it has a lot to do with the black eye I'm sporting that matches his dad's. "What position do you play?"

"Center."

"Cool. Me, too."

He straightens, his interest piquing. "You play?"

"Yep. Been playing as long as your dad. He was my left wing," I add, unable to help myself.

"Nice try, asshole. More like you were mine," Sawyer cuts in, stepping out of the house.

Perfect timing.

"Sawyer, watch your mouth," Grace scolds, following out behind him.

Hope walks up to him with her hand out. "That's five dollars for the swear jar, Daddy."

His hard gaze moves from me down to his daughter and instantly softens. "Since when has it been five bucks?"

"Since I'm saving for the new Holiday Barbie."

Yep, she's definitely my kind of girl.

Reaching down, he sweeps her legs out from under her and hangs her upside down. She giggles as he lifts her to face level. "How about you take that pie back you gave him and I'll buy you that Barbie myself."

"Sorry, Daddy, but that wouldn't be very polite."

Clearly, her manners come from her mother.

She takes his face between both of her little hands. "But you know you own my heart."

He grunts but kisses her before flipping her right side up and placing her to her feet.

"All right, come on, you two," Grace says, waving the kids in. "Let's go back inside and leave Mr. Jase and your dad to talk."

"Okay, Mama," Hope complies before turning back to me. "It was nice to meet you, Mr. Jase."

"You too, Hope Catherine Evans…and you, Parker."

Parker nods back, seeming a little more receptive than when he first walked out.

"Play nice, Daddy," Hope says, patting his arm before walking with her mother into the house.

I cock a brow at him. "Your kids are nice, clearly they take after your wife."

Okay, that probably wasn't the best way to start this conversation, but I can't help myself. This is not fucking easy.

"What the fuck are you doing here, Crawford?" he asks, ignoring the dig.

"We need to talk."

"I have nothing to say to you."

"Then you can listen because I have a lot to say to you."

His eyes narrow. "You think because you're fucking my sister you can come to my house, talk shit, and think I'm going to listen?"

I tense, my self-control starting to slip. "If you don't want fists flying in front of your kids, I suggest you watch what you say when it comes to Sam and me."

"Did I say something that isn't true? Your exact words were '*pay-back*.'"

Guilt settles over my chest, heavy and hard. "Look, I didn't mean what I said the other day. I was pissed off and ran my mouth."

"You think that makes it okay?"

"No, I don't. But I'm here to tell you that I'm in love with her, and I'm not going anywhere. So you're just going to have to deal with it."

"You're fucking crazy if you think I'm going to let you near my sister again."

"That's not up to you. She's a big girl and can make her own decisions."

"I disagree. She hasn't made the best decisions when it comes to men."

I stiffen, returning his glare. "Are you comparing me to that bastard ex of hers?"

He shrugs, crossing his arms. "If the shoe fits."

I shoot out of my chair, anger burning in my blood, rich and thick. "I'd never put my fucking hands on her and you know it!"

He takes a step toward me. "The hell I do. You have a fucking vendetta against me because of Stephanie and you are trying to use my sister to do it."

"This has nothing to do with that bitch, or you for that matter. This is about Sam and me!"

"Stop it!" Grace storms out of the house, placing herself between us. "You both need to calm down, the kids can hear you."

We glare at one another, our chests heaving with fury.

"Look, both of you need to cut the shit," she starts. "This is not about your stupid grudge. This is about Sam. *She* is what's important. You hear me, Sawyer?"

He rears back, affronted. "Why the hell are you only calling me out?"

"Because he made an effort by coming here and you're acting like an ass!"

That's right!

I cross my arms over my chest, enjoying his torment. That's until she speaks again.

"You've seen her this past week, Sawyer," she says quietly, her anger diminishing. "She's heartbroken and hasn't stopped crying."

The thought has my chest constricting painfully. Is it because she's missing me as much as I am her? Or is it because I'm an asshole and she thinks I don't love her?

I'm praying it's not the latter.

"Fix this." She points at him, her voice hardening again. "Or...or...

No more pie for you!" Without another word she storms back inside, slamming the door behind her.

"Thanks a lot, asshole," he snaps. "It wasn't enough to come between my sister and me now you have to stir shit up with my wife."

"I didn't stir up shit with your wife. You did that because you're an asshole."

"I'm not an asshole, you're an asshole!"

"Oh yeah?"

"Yeah!"

"Well you better get used to this asshole because I'm going to marry your sister."

"The hell you are."

"Yep. I am. I even have your parents' blessing."

"Fuck that! They did not."

I smile smugly. "Sure did."

"Buuull—shit."

I shrug. "Believe what you want but it's true."

He starts to look unsure. "Yeah, well, even if it is my sister can still say no."

"She could, but I'll just keep asking until she says yes."

"Is that so?"

"Yep. I told you I don't plan on going anywhere."

"Gotta go home sometime, Crawford," he tosses back with a smirk.

"I am home."

The cocky smile slips from his face. "What the hell are you talking about?"

"I'm moving here," I tell him with a broad smile, happy to deliver the news. "I start my new job at the Charleston Fire Department in two weeks."

If Sam says yes that is, but I keep that part to myself.

"No fucking way. You are not moving here. This is my goddamn town."

I grunt at the ridiculous statement. This fucker would be the worst mayor ever.

"What exactly is pissing you off?" I ask, fed up with the back and forth. "Is this really about Sam or is this about you and me?"

"Of course it's about you and me. I don't fucking trust you."

"If I wanted to use Sam to get back at you, I would have done it long ago."

He glares at me but remains silent.

"You might not like me, but you know me," I push on. "I don't fucking play like that."

He leans against the banister behind him, arms crossing over his chest again. "You should have come to us when you saw him hit her," he says, steering the conversation in another direction.

Now I realize why he's being a bigger prick than usual. "So that's what you're really pissed about. Because I didn't call you?"

"If you cared about her, you would have come to us."

"Fuck that! That's Sam's business, not mine."

"It became yours when you witnessed it," he snaps.

"Exactly, and that's why I kicked his ass. I dealt with it *my* way."

"Did you stop to think maybe I wanted to kick his ass? She's my sister!"

"Well you weren't fucking there. I was," I bellow, anger rising hot and fast as I remember that night. The fateful moment that changed everything between us. "Are you seriously mad I kicked some guy's ass for hitting your sister?"

"No. I'm pissed off that someone put their hands on her to begin with, and I'm also pissed off that when I go to kick his ass it's going to have less meaning because you already did it."

"Well, I was there, and I plan to always be there. I'll never let any-one hurt her again. Which is why we need to figure this shit out because I won't cause her pain."

"You won't if you leave."

I shake my head, frustrated. "You don't get it. I'm not going any-where. I love her, and I plan to fight for her until my last fucking breath."

His jaw locks down stubbornly.

"Just give me a chance. I'm not saying you have to like it. She's your sister, I get that. But respect it. For no one else's sake but hers."

Silence stretches between us as he glares back at me. A few beats pass before I witness a small shred of acceptance cross his face.

Pushing from the banister, he steps closer to me, getting in my personal space. "If you're lying to me and you hurt her, I will fucking kill you. Do you understand?"

It takes every ounce of self-control I possess not to push back. Instead, I give a tight nod but add, "Two-way street, Evans. Brother or not, if you hurt her I'll kick your ass...again."

He grunts. "You did not kick my ass last time. I kicked yours."

"Your eye is worse than mine."

"The hell it is."

"It is, and as much as I'd love to stand around and debate about it, I have better things to do." I clap him on the shoulder. "We'll discuss it at the next family supper. I can't wait to try some of your wife's pie." Smirking, I descend the steps.

"I swear you have a fucking death wish, Crawford," he calls to my retreating back. "And my sister has to say yes first, asshole."

He's right. However, I don't plan on taking no for an answer.

CHAPTER 22

Sam

My hands are shoved in the pockets of my knee length skirt as I walk home from spending the afternoon exploring Charleston. Sitting around the house was driving me crazy, I needed a distraction. But as much as I loved seeing what this beautiful city has to offer, it did little to ease my conflicted heart.

I'm beginning to think my mom is right and I need to call Jase. I need the closure but the problem is I don't want it.

I want him.

I just don't know how we could ever make it work, not when his hatred for my brother runs so deep.

Sighing, I turn down my street and decide when I get home I'm going to head over to my brother's for a visit. If anyone can cheer me up it's my darling niece and nephew. It's also time I face Sawyer. He called last night, wanting to come over because Mom had called him after our talk but I just couldn't. I was too emotionally drained after telling my mom everything about Grant and Jase; I didn't have it in me to do it again so soon. I'm sure my father and Sawyer are already plotting Grant's death, something I need to make sure doesn't happen. Not for Grant's sake but theirs.

As I make it to my driveway, I come to a quick stop and frown at the tipped over basket of peaches spilled all over the place.

"What on earth…" I walk up the paved concrete, my heart beginning to thunder as I kneel down next to the strewn fruit and find a note dangling from a piece of white ribbon tied to the handle of the basket.

My hands tremble as I pull it off and unfold it. As I read the words written on the paper, the world stops around me.

All the reasons I love peaches.

They're sweet and soft. Vibrant and fresh. They stand out boldly amongst all the other meager fruits because they are the prettiest.
   They're perfect.
   They are also loyal and grow best when surrounded by family.
   This must be why I fell in love with a girl who smells just like them, looks like them, and tastes like them.
   I've also heard they are very forgiving and give second chances. I'm hoping this is true because I've come to realize I can't live without peaches.
   I need them to survive.
   I need you.

Tears stream down my cheeks, blurring the last of the words in front of me. Noticing a trail of peaches wrapping around my house, I follow them and find Jase sitting on my front steps, holding a small wrapped gift box. My hand covers my mouth, stifling the sob that escapes when he flashes me his sexy smirk.

"Hey, Peaches," he greets me, rising to his feet.

"What are you doing here?"

He walks down the steps, stopping just in front of me. "I came to see you." His large hands cup my cheeks, the touch sending my fragile heart into an emotional tailspin. "Can we talk?"

Unable to speak, I nod, leading him up the steps and into my house. I'm aware of how close he is when we enter, that ever-present pull between us more profound than ever. Dropping my purse on the counter, I spin around and find him standing a few feet away. Close enough to smell. Close enough to touch.

"Can I get you something?" I ask, my voice raw from the emotion threatening to suffocate me.

He shakes his head. "You're all I need right now."

My heart warms yet yearns for more. So many words hang between us. I desperately want to tell him how much I've missed him and how I haven't stopped thinking about him since I left, but I swallow the confession.

"You look good," he remarks softly.

"You're a terrible liar. I'm a total mess." I swipe at my tear-stained cheeks, knowing my mascara is probably everywhere right now.

His steps are purposeful as he closes the distance between us. Placing the gift he's holding on the counter, he plants both hands on either side of me, his powerful body crowding mine against the sink. My breathing turns shallow, his close proximity wreaking havoc on my senses and heart.

Leaning in, he trails his nose across my damp cheek. "You're the prettiest mess I've ever seen."

I bite my trembling lip, my fingers curling into his shirt as I fight the need to drag him closer and soak in his warmth. I've missed him so much it hurts.

"I'm sorry, Sam." His sincere apology is nothing more than a whisper but it has the power to heal so much. "So fucking sorry for what I said. I didn't mean it. You have to believe me."

My eyes drift closed, my heart breaking at the painful memory. "I do believe you, but it doesn't stop it from hurting any less."

"I know, and I'll regret it for the rest of my life. But, if you give me a chance, I promise to make it right. I can't lose you."

"I don't want to lose you either." I swallow hard, trying to contain my emotions. "But I'm at a loss, Jase. I can't choose between you two. I love you both too much."

His arms come around me, holding my shattered pieces together. "You don't have to choose, baby. I'd never make you do that."

I shake my head, not understanding how he can say that when they've made it clear I can't have them both.

His fingers curl beneath my chin, lifting my eyes to his. "I went and saw him today," he tells me, his thumb swiping away my flowing tears.

I still, hope flaring inside of me. "Sawyer?"

He nods. "After I saw your parents."

Complete and utter shock rolls through me.

"You have a nice family. I especially enjoyed meeting your niece and nephew."

My breath hitches on a sob. "You met Hope and Parker?"

"Yeah. They're nice kids, even though they tried feeding me Asshole Pie from your brother."

A watery laugh escapes me. I can only imagine how awkward that was for him. I feel bad he was alone to deal with it, but he doesn't seem bothered by it, if his sexy grin is any indication.

His expression softens as he reaches up to stroke the edge of my smile. I place my hand over his and lean into his touch, feeling the cracks of my soul beginning to heal.

"We had a good talk and came to an understanding," he continues. "We found something that we both agree on."

"What's that?"

"Your happiness."

Warmth explodes through me; warming the cold and empty space I've had inside of me this past week.

He rests his forehead on mine. "I love you much more than I ever hated him."

Hot tears track down my face as he finally says the words I've longed to hear. "I love you too, so much." Wrapping my arms around his neck, I bury my face in his shoulder and cry. His familiar scent invades me, soothing my fragile composure.

He picks me up off my feet, hugging me tight, before placing me on the counter and coming to stand between my legs. Reaching up, he brushes a piece of my hair out of my face. "I'd do anything to make you happy, Sam. That's all I care about."

The love and devotion in his eyes makes my heart leap. I know he means every word. Not just by the conviction in his voice, but the fact that he made peace with Sawyer proves it, too.

Picking the gift back up, he brings it between us. I accept it with a smile. "What's this?"

"Open it."

Plucking the red silk ribbon that's wrapped around the box, I remove the lid and push aside the mounds of tissue paper to unveil a beautiful peach ornament made entirely of glass.

With shaking hands, I carefully reach inside and pull it out, my breath freezing in my lungs when I discover a ring attached to the stem.

My watery eyes shoot up to his, hope filling my chest.

"I've done a lot of thinking this past week," he starts, removing the ring from the stem. "And I've come to realize that Madam Juju might not be such a whack job after all."

His comment takes me by surprise but I can't help but smile. "Why do you say that?"

His warm eyes hold me captive, rendering me speechless and helpless to this incredible hold he has on me. "Because I know, without a doubt, that I loved you before I ever met you."

"Oh." My breath catches on a sob. It's all I can manage at the moment.

"I left it all behind, Sam," he says, confusing me. "My job, my life back in Colorado. I left it all. I start at the Charleston Fire Department in two weeks."

"Jase, no," I breathe. "You don't have to do that. We can talk about it. We'll work something out. We—"

He presses a finger to my lips, silencing me. "Nothing matters more than your happiness, and I know how much it means for you to be here with your family."

"Yes, it does, but your family is important too, and I won't take that from you."

He shrugs. "My family will come visit and we can go back there. It's not as important to me as it is to you."

I shake my head, guilt plaguing me. "I can't do this to you. I can't take that away from you."

"You're not taking anything from me, baby. I'm gaining so much more," he says, making me fall in love with him all over again. "You're all I need, Sam. Just you forever and I'll be happy."

Taking my left hand, he slides the ring on my finger, and it fits so perfectly that I swear it was made just for me.

"Marry me." He leans in close, his breath tickling my lips. "Marry me or I will have no friends here."

I burst out laughing, tears of joy spilling down my cheeks.

His smile fades as he rests his forehead on mine. "Say yes, Sam."

I wrap my arms around his neck, pulling him as close as he can get. "Yes, I'll marry you. Nothing would make me happier than to be yours forever."

He flashes me that sexy smile of his. "You are way better at words than me, baby."

His mouth seals over mine, effectively cutting off my giggle. The kiss is deep and soul shattering. My fingers thread through his hair while his slip beneath my skirt, his touch setting my skin on fire.

I moan into his mouth and lock my legs around his lean waist, needing him more than my next breath.

With a growl, he cups my bottom and lifts me from the counter. "Where's your room?"

"Down the hall, last door on the right," I mumble against his lips, our heated mouths never severing as he carries me to the bedroom. He lowers me onto my mattress, his heavy weight settling over top of me as his skillful tongue coaxes mine, fueling my hunger. A stark, ravishing hunger that only he can bring out of me.

We waste no time tearing at each other's clothes, our hands urgent, each of us desperate for the other. Pleasure steals my breath when I feel his heated skin upon mine.

"Oh god, I missed this. I missed you," I cry, my fingers digging into his strong shoulders.

"I missed you too, baby. So fucking much."

I lift my hips, seeking more of him, needing him inside of me. "Jase, now. Please, I need you."

A harsh groan rumbles from him, vibrating against my lips. "I wanted to take my time with you, taste every inch of you that I've missed this past week, but fuck it. We have forever for that."

"Yes, forever," I breathe, my heart soaring at the thought.

With swift precision, he rolls us over, positioning me on top of him. "Ride me, baby. Show me how much you missed me."

I quickly obey. Aligning myself above his hard cock, I sink down on him. My head falls back on a blissful moan as he completes me, body and soul.

"Jesus, Sam," he grits between clenched teeth, his fingers digging into my hips.

"It's always so good."

"Always, baby. It's like coming home. I don't ever want to be anywhere else."

His words light up my soul. He is home.

My home.

His hips pump up, burying his cock deep inside of me. A harsh whimper parts my lips, my nails raking across his muscular chest as the most exquisite sensations whip through me.

"Tell me you love me. Tell me you're mine forever," he demands, sheer dominance filling his expression as he keeps his pace, relentless with every thrust.

I smile down at him. "I'm madly in love with you, Jase Crawford, and am yours forever."

"That's right, baby, and I'm going to fill this hungry pussy every day. Sometimes slow and sometimes fast, but it will always be me."

"Always."

He moves a hand between us, running his knuckle through my slick heat, finding the bundle of pulsing nerves.

A heated whimper breaches my lips. Grabbing his wrist, I ride against the pressure of his hand. "Jase. I'm going to come."

"Yeah, you are, and it's going to feel so fucking good on my cock." He switches the angle of his thrusts, sending me over the steep edge.

Ecstasy explodes through me like a violent storm, stealing my breath and washing through me like a tidal wave. Reaching up, he hooks a hand behind my neck and pulls me down to swallow my cries, his greedy mouth inhaling everything I have to give him. He doesn't hold back and follows along with me.

Our bodies merge, souls tethering together by a love so strong, so powerful, neither one of us ever stood a chance against it.

Afterward, we lie together, my cheek on Jase's hard chest, a feeling of contentment settling over me with the calming sound of his steady heartbeat.

"I still can't believe you're here," I whisper. "That you came for me."

"I'll always come for you."

Peace wraps around me like a blanket, heavy and warm. His strong hand moves over mine where it lays on his stomach. Lifting it in the air between us, his thumb smooths over the ring on my finger. "We're going to have a good life, Sam. I promise."

I turn his hand palm up and bring it next to mine. Our fingers instantly curl, displaying the heart that only we create. "Yeah, we are."

He drops a kiss on the top of my head and it's not long before I feel his breathing even out. Before letting myself follow along with him, I slip out from under his strong arm and throw on my robe before tiptoeing to the kitchen. Digging through my purse on the counter, I grab my cell phone out and call Sawyer.

He answers on the first ring. "You're calling to tell me you said yes, aren't you?"

His grumpy voice doesn't deter the smile on my face. "I'm calling to tell you that I love you and to say thank you."

There's a long moment of silence before he speaks again.

"I just want you to be happy, Sam. I don't ever want to see you hurt the way you did this week. Not ever again."

My throat clogs with tears. "He makes me happy. So happy."

"Then that's all that matters."

I smile, my heart bursting at the seams with love for all of the men in my life.

"Can you do me a favor though? Just this once?"

"What?" I ask, willing to do anything for him.

"Give him one good punch in the nuts for me. Just one."

Except that.

Rolling my eyes, I burst out laughing. "Good-bye, Sawyer."

He grunts but it's half-hearted. "I love you, Sam."

"I love you, too," I whisper back.

Hanging up, I crawl back in bed with Jase, making sure to be as quiet as possible. I can't resist brushing a soft kiss across his lips before lifting his arm and resuming my spot once again, my head resting on his chest. Lifting my chin, I gaze up at his handsome face, loving that I will get to see this every night for the rest of my life.

I know with every fiber of my being, no matter how many lives I live, or where I go after this one, we will always find each other.

EPILOGUE

Rose

September 2, 1869

We met in a peach grove. I had been out picking to make jam when he appeared out of nowhere. He was tall, dark, and handsome, but most of all, mysterious.

He arrived in town six months ago and was supposed to be just passing through, but days turned into weeks then eventually months. Many of the town's folk were wary and didn't trust him, but the day I met Joshua Lawson, my lonely existence changed forever.

The first moment our eyes connected, my breath was stolen. Then, he smiled at me and my heart stopped beating altogether. I will never forget the first words he said to me.

"Peaches and a pretty girl. My two favorite things."

My stomach dipped and a shy smile had stolen my lips, but I did my best to hide the effect he casted upon me. "I guess what the women in town are saying about you is true."

His dashing grin had spread even wider, making the spot between my legs tingle. It had made me blush furiously. "Depends what you've heard. I am quite charming."

Bold and arrogant had been more like it, but yes, that was what the women in town had said. Many of them. It was a cold reminder of why I had to leave before I fell under the same spell. The feelings I experienced in that moment were wrong.

Without so much as a dignified reply, I picked up my basket and gave him my most polite smile. I was a lady, after all. "Good day, Mr. Lawson."

Awareness prickled my skin when I had brushed past him.

I didn't make it far before he called out after me. "Don't believe everything you hear, Miss Emerson. None of those women in town are near as beautiful as you are."

Butterflies danced in my tummy when I realized he knew my name.

That was our first encounter and it wasn't our last. I had gone back every day after and he was always there, waiting for me. With his charming smile and quick wit. I fell for him instantly.

It all started with subtle looks and touches. He had familiar eyes that felt like home. They were welcoming and warm. He also made me laugh and that was something I didn't do often. Not anymore. Not since losing my entire family when I was only ten years old in a train derailment.

We spent a lot of time together in that grove and quite a few nights, too. The first time we met I knew we shared something special, something indescribable. But the first time we kissed, it was as if our souls had become one. Then he made love to me under a star-covered sky, and I knew I'd never be the same again.

It was the most beautiful time of my life, yet it was also a sin because I've been promised to another man. A terrible man who's cruel and does not know what it means to really love someone.

My uncle took me in after I lost my family and promised me to his business partner's eldest son, Kenneth Harold the third. Our marriage arrangement had nothing to do with love.

"It's what's best for the family." My uncle always said.

Closing my eyes, I think about the night I told Joshua I was being forced to marry another. I'll never forget the anger in his eyes. The possession. And his vow to me.

"I swear I'll never let that happen. You are mine, Rose. You always have been. You always will be."

Oh, how I long to be with him now. To have him hold me in his arms. To hear his voice, but instead I lie in bed the night before my wedding, tears of sorrow soaking my pillow.

Kenneth and my uncle found out about us and moved the wedding up to tomorrow. I searched all evening for Joshua, frantic and scared, only to find out he left town this morning after being paid a visit from my uncle. I can only imagine what was said to make him leave without saying good-bye.

The thought has me crying harder.

It wasn't supposed to end like this. I was supposed to have time. Time to find a way out of this loveless deal.

A sudden bang sounds from downstairs and pulls me out of my turmoil. It's so loud it vibrates my bedroom walls.

"Rose!"

I sit up quickly, trying to dispel my despair long enough to hear the commotion beyond my door.

"Get the hell out of my house!" my uncle yells.

"I'm not leaving here without her."

Joshua.

Relief floods my body as a sob of joy tumbles from my lips. I dash from the bed, lifting my white cotton nightgown as I descend the winding staircase. I halt mid-step when I see Joshua standing over my uncle who is lying on the floor with blood trickling from his lip.

"Joshua," I breathe. My mind is still trying to catch up with everything that is happening but my heart settles on the man before me, his dark eyes filled with love and determination.

"Don't marry him. Come with me instead."

"Where?" I ask.

"Chicago."

My eyes widen in shock, a sliver of fear creeping up my spine for the unknown.

"The train leaves in thirty minutes. I have a job lined up at the fire department there." He closes the distance between us, coming to stand at the bottom of the stairs. "I love you, Rose. I want to build a life with you. I want you to have my children. I want to wake up to your beautiful face every day for the rest of my life."

Tears stain my cheeks and a smile dances across my lips. It vanishes though the moment I meet my uncle's furious gaze.

"If you leave here with him, you leave with nothing but the clothes on your back. You will lose everything, including your place in this family."

"I lost my family long ago," I choke out. "I've been nothing but an obligation to you and you know it."

"I've done right by you!"

"You are forcing me to marry a man I don't love."

"It's what's best for you," he bellows. "I mean it. Leave here and you will lose it all."

I turn back to Joshua and find him watching me, his dark eyes strong and filled with promise. He extends his hand to me. "Trust me, Rose."

Those three words seal my fate.

Smiling, I take his hand, my heart leaping with anticipation, excitement, and yes, love. I knew I was gaining so much more than I was losing.

"Don't you ever come back, Rose! You hear me?"

I ignore my uncle's furious voice and run behind Joshua, trying to keep up with his fast strides. The night air is warm as we make it outside and bound down the porch steps. I smile as the cool grass tickles my bare feet, the taste of freedom teasing my heart as we flee our past to start our future.

Joshua stops halfway across the lawn and pulls me in for a soul-shattering kiss. I wrap my arms around his neck, my tears of joy mixing with our passion as he lifts me off my feet.

"I can't believe you came back for me." My heart is so full, nearly bursting at the seams with love for this man.

He places me back on my feet, his strong hands framing my face as he pulls back to look at me. "I'll always come for you."

They are words I'll remember forever.

"Are we really doing this?" I ask with a laugh.

He quirks a brow. "Second thoughts?"

I shake my head. "Never."

He graces me with that charming smile. The same one that melted my heart all those months ago when we first met. The same one I can't imagine living without.

"We're going to have a good life, Rose. I promise."

I reach up and cup his strong jaw. "I know."

"We'll get you new clothes as soon as we arrive. Anything you need," he promises.

"As long as I have you, I have everything I need."

He gives me one more toe-curling kiss before we head to the train station, catching it just in the nick of time.

We made it to Chicago safely and were married in a small ceremony shortly after we arrived. We couldn't wait to start our lives together. Joshua supported us, working as a firefighter, and I found a job as a teacher in a local school. We were happy. We made love often and laughed everyday. We were ready to start our family.

But fate had robbed us of our destiny. Two years later, the Great Chicago Fire took three hundred souls, including my beloved husband. But the child he sacrificed his own life to save, lived. Because of him.

I lost so much more that day than the man I loved. I lost a piece of my soul forever. I never remarried. I knew I would never be able to love someone the way I did Joshua. Even knowing our outcome, I will never regret the decision I made that night to leave with him. Those two years were the best of my life. Every second I had with him was magic. I lived in the memories we created together and carried them with me into eternity.

It wouldn't be until 2016 when the stars realigned and fate had its say once more for Joshua and Rose. Samantha and Jase lived a long and happy life together, building the family they'd always dreamed of and sharing a love that would span many lifetimes to come. Soul mates until their dying days, only to find each other somewhere down the road once again.

Most likely…in another peach grove.

The End...for now.

Make sure to check out my website www.authorkclynn.com for what's coming next.

Acknowledgements

I'm blessed to have so many amazing people who love and support me in this beautiful journey I'm on. Most of them have been with me from the very beginning. They've had my back, believed in me, and wouldn't let me give up when times were daunting.

To everyone who has been a part of this amazing journey with me—family, my beautiful editor, betas, friends, my author groups, bloggers, and readers around the world. You know who you are. Thank you. I love and cherish every single one of you.

A special shout-out to the brave men of Fire Station Two and Captain Gyepesi aka Captain Gypsi, who so graciously allowed me to be a part of the family for a night. I found you funny and admirable. I knew the moment I met you, I would make you the captain in my series.

Thank you to the rest of you for the courageous, honorable work you do and for welcoming me into your station. An extended thanks to Kevin Royle for continuing to answer any questions I have and extending an open invitation to the station. I appreciate it more than you know.

You men are true heroes.

About the Author

K.C. Lynn is a small town girl living in Western Canada. She grew up in a family of four children—two sisters and a brother. Her mother was the lady who baked homemade goods for everyone on the street and her father was a respected man who worked in the RCMP. He's since retired and now works for the criminal justice system. This being one of the things that inspires K.C. to write romantic suspense about the trials and triumphs of our heroes.

K.C. married her high school sweetheart and they started a big family of their own—two adorable girls and a set of handsome twin boys. They still reside in the same small town but K.C.'s heart has always longed for the south, where everyone says 'y'all' and eats biscuits and gravy for breakfast.

It was her love for romance books that gave K.C. the courage to sit down and write her own novel. It was then a beautiful world opened up and she found what she was meant to do…write.

When K.C.'s not spending time with her beautiful family she can be found in her writing cave, living in the fabulous minds of her characters and their stories.

Made in the USA
Columbia, SC
08 September 2018